Secrets,

Snapdragons,

and a Spirit

Also by Tina D.C. Hayes

No More Tears

ROCK CANDY ROMANTIC SUSPENSE
Nefarious

PETAL PUSHERS MYSTERY SERIES
Poison, Perennials, and a Poltergeist

Secrets,

Snapdragons,

and a Spirit

Petal Pushers Mystery Series, Book 2

Tina D. C. Hayes

Hazy Moon Ink

ISBN-13: 978-0692362198
ISBN-10: 0692362193

2nd Edition

Hazy Moon Ink

Prologue

It's so nice to visit with my dearest friend again after all this time, but I swany, I cain't figure out what the devil she's a-goin' on about, or why her girls aren't with her. Poor woman is a little addled, but after all she's been through, I guess that's understandable. Or maybe she was jokin' around about that one part. I mean, do I look like the kind of fool who believes in ghosts?

The rest is comin' through clear as a bell. I swore I'd keep her secret all those years ago, but if she's ready to face the past, I'll stick by her side the whole way, help her the best I can.

I wanted to wear the pin she gave me, but couldn't find it this morning. My Hattie was playin' dress up with it last I remember, but I know she'll take good care of it.

Oh me. There's nary a dull minute around this place, what with me watchin' over Darci, tendin' to the plants, and now I reckon things are about to *get even busier. Folks are dependin' on me to set things right, so heaven help anybody who dares to stop us.*

Chapter One

*The flowers of late winter and early spring occupy
places in our hearts well out of
proportion to their size.*
~ Gertrude S. Wister

The first day of spring had shown up on the calendar a few weeks before, Darci's favorite time of year, when green grass shoots through brown undergrowth and gardeners get to play in the yard again.

She unzipped her jacket as the early morning air warmed up. For the second year in a row she'd resolved to lose weight, and so far she'd stuck to her new routine of walking two miles a day, weather permitting. April was so much more comfortable than the cold snap last month, when she'd trudged home through the snow with a runny nose, feeling like her frozen lungs were about to burst.

Darci picked up her pace as a car drove past,

leaving her in a wake of gas fumes. "That vehicle needed a tune-up or something." She covered her nose with a Kleenex and waved her other hand in front of her face. The fresh air was now tainted with carbon emissions, and her hair would probably stink all day unless she got home in time to take a quick shower before work. As her Nikes trekked along the blacktop, she decided that if she hurried, she might be able to swing by Krispy Kreme to treat herself to just one cream-filled chocolate glazed donut. Her mouth watered and she could almost smell the fresh baked pastry.

The hum of tires on asphalt approached from behind, so she stepped closer to the edge of the little country road. The 'toot, toot, toot' of the horn let her know who the driver was before he pulled alongside her and let the window down.

"Mornin, Jimbo. What are you doing out and about this early?" Darci asked her cousin-in-law as she leaned against the door. "Oh, now I see." She reached in to tweak baby Cole's rosy little nose.

"Thought I'd let Charlotte sleep in. This little guy's been up since about five o'clock. Again. Taking him for a ride is about the only thing that calms him down, and when we're lucky, brings on a nap. Those frozen plastic baby Popsicle things don't do much good." He shook his head, but then winked. "Don't see why she won't let me put whiskey on his gums like my folks did when I was teething."

Darci started to remind him that that was way before medical science and common sense pre-

4

vailed, and countless studies warned people not to get their teething babies all liquored up, but stopped herself, since she was fairly sure he knew better. "Try some teething biscuits. They'll look disgusting after he slobbers on 'em a while, but they should help." She tweaked Cole's foot again.

"Will do. Guess we'll let you get back to your walk. You'll probably pass us, since we're just killing time til his mommy gets up." Jimbo put the car back in gear. "See you later."

Darci picked her pace up, hoping to get her heart to cardio level. Movement near her feet drew her attention. She jumped back and screamed. What she'd at first taken to be a ribbon or a slice of blown tire slithered across the road, right in front of her.

"Jimbo! Ahhhh!" The ribbon paused to lift its head and look at her. "Come back! Help!" Darci hopped from one foot to the other, since her fear of stepping any closer to the snake overpowered her urge to run full speed ahead. She waved, hopped, and hollered, hoping that if he looked back in the rearview mirror he would understand she needed help, not think she was swatting a bee and doing jumping jacks at the same time. "Snake!"

Grandma Odette always said those creepy-crawlies were bad omens of evil, enemies, or death, but right now the prospect of getting bitten was the most horrifying thing Darci could imagine.

The snake was almost to the other side of the

road, probably fixing to take a bath in the ditch, the little bastard, when the truck's brake lights came on. Darci took a deep breath, then bolted for the pickup as fast her legs would carry her, yelling "Snake!" the whole way.

At work later that morning, Darci leaned against Petal Pushers' back door and watched the construction going on in the yard. Last year business had done well enough that she'd decided to expand a little by adding a second greenhouse. No decision ever came easy for her, and she hated to have a big expense hanging over her head, but after much thought and practically begging Wade and Charlotte to talk her out of it, she moved forward with the project. She'd nearly puked on her shoes at the thought of adding to the business loan; she couldn't stand the idea of starting back at square one, since she'd paid it down so much, so she took out a separate loan against the equity. Wade offered to float the money to her, but should have known better. This flower shop was her responsibility and lifelong dream, and sink or swim, she was determined to do it herself.

The project should be done in just a couple more days. With the extra veggies, herbs, and flowers she hoped to grow in the thing, she felt pretty confident, most of the time, that she'd be able to pay off the expense within the next couple of years. She'd make double and triple payments after it started making money in late spring.

"Well Daisy," she said to the shop mascot as she turned around, "I better get back to work instead of daydreaming or I never will get anything paid for."

The parakeet tweeted in agreement.

Darci paused to run her fingers over the mosaic clock that hung in a place of honor on the wall. It reminded her that anything was possible.

She sat down at her desk to open the mail. Those heirloom tomato seeds she ordered should be in soon, and that's what she hoped to find as she flipped through the electric bill, a car lot ad, a couple sale fliers, and a bank statement. When she came to an envelope addressed to a familiar name that wasn't her own, she gasped. The rest of the mail in her hand dropped to the desk.

She couldn't believe her eyes.

Petal Pushers used to be a regular home, vacant for years before Darci purchased it to house her flower shop. After some research last fall, she'd learned quite a bit about the previous residents. Adelaide Brown had lived there until she died in 1941.

How weird this was, to get a letter addressed to 'The Family of Addie Brown', someone who died over seventy years ago. It must be a very old acquaintance, one who'd kept the Brown's old address.

She swiveled her chair around, deep in thought, the handwritten envelope held to her chest. The mosaic clock on the wall drew her attention again, the one she'd made a few months ago from a broken plate found in one of the walls, a Brown family heirloom. The project had been Miss Addie's idea.

No two ways about it, Darci had to open it. "Miss Addie," she said aloud, glad to be the only one currently in the shop. Charlotte and Hoyt had both seen the ghost, and she suspected Wade had too, since he abruptly stopped making fun of her and Charlotte for mentioning the haunting. Her son Paxton even had an encounter with the Ghost Lady, as they'd referred to her before learning her name, but the boy thought she was a Mennonite because of her long dress, and no way was Darci going to explain the real situation to him. "Looks like somebody sent you a letter."

A cold spot settled over her, something she'd gotten used to over the past year. Daisy tweeted happily, as she always did when the ghost was around.

"I'll open it and read it out loud." After wielding her letter opener, she glanced around the room, took a deep breath, and then carefully unfolded the letter.

Dear Brown Family,

It is our sincere hope that this letter finds the family of Mrs. Adelaide Brown, my great-grandmother's dear friend. My great-grandmother last contacted Addie in the early nineteen-forties at this address.

Betsy McGee was my great-grandmother. On her deathbed, she revealed circumstances that occurred at my grandmother and great-aunt's birth (they're identical twins), and about their father's identity. Addie Brown was the midwife who saved the babies' lives after a difficult birth. It appears, if Betsy was not confused, that she learned, many years later, of an inheritance left to my great-grandfather's heirs, but she feared for her daughters' lives and her own if they claimed it while certain people were still alive. She said she changed her name when she left Webster County so their father's people couldn't track them down, thinking they would hurt the twins or take them away from her. I don't know why she believed this, but my grandmother was adamant her mother was in her right mind, even as she spoke her last words. The good lord took her before she could mention our true family surname, or explain the rest of the story.

I'm writing in hopes that some of Addie's people can recall something, anything that might help find the missing pieces to this strange puzzle. I know it's a long shot, but maybe it's possible some of the letters my Great-Granny mailed to her may be in a scrapbook or tucked away in some of her mementos. Surely whatever tragic event this was took place in your town, so there must be some records in Dixon that might shine a little light on the subject.

It was Betsy's dying wish for us to claim what she said was our rightful inheritance and understand why she did what she did, though she passed before she could explain exactly what that was. Obviously, it is doubtful any monetary allotment is still around after all these years, though she thought there was. What my brother and cousins and I want is to know the truth, to find out about the branch of our family that was hidden from us.

Of course, my great-grandmother Betsy passed away decades ago and her daughters died in their nineties, within a few months of each other. They didn't pursue their mother's request because they worried about what they might find. Toward the end of their lives they regretted that decision and began to look for answers. On their last birthday together, they made their children promise to carry out Betsy's dying wish, to claim the inheritance if there actually is any, and find out the truth. My mother only recently passed this information on to

10

me, the first I'd heard of it, and that's what has led me to write this letter.

If you're reading this and aren't familiar with the people I've mentioned, maybe you could pass it on to some of the Browns in town. Any help would be so greatly appreciated.

Sincerely,
Ellen Morgan

The paper shook in Darci's hand as she reread the letter. Interesting was much too mild an adjective, under the circumstances. Darci had learned a lot about the life of her resident ghost last October when Miss Addie's granddaughter came to the shop for a nostalgic visit.

A million thoughts spun inside her mind. Betsy and the twins! She remembered Hattie mentioning them on her visit. She said Betsy gave Addie a pin for saving her babies. Hadn't she said Betsy was Cherokee?

Darci sensed excitement in the coldness. Damn shame Miss Addie couldn't communicate with them verbally, since she'd surely be able to answer all of Ellen's questions. But she did seem to be able to put ideas in Darci's head, like last year when she had the sudden urge to rush to the library to research the deed just days before the ghost's granddaughter showed up on her doorstep, and when she'd named the parakeet, Miss Addie's favorite flower just happened to pop into her mind. Other than that, the ghost had a

11

practiced talent for knocking over books and could move small objects.

With the letter very carefully folded and safely tucked away in her drawer, Darci stood and walked to the porthole shaped window. She fidgeted with her wedding ring, lost in thought as she looked out over shoots of new grass barely visible under last year's crunchy brown groundcover. How difficult it must have been for Betsy, on the run so long ago with two baby girls. Starting over in a new town in that situation today would be hard enough, but a widow having to support herself in a strange place and raise her children, all the time living in fear of whatever it was that made her leave Webster County in the first place must have been unbearable.

She sighed. Darci's own father had died when she was thirteen. Her mom had a hard enough time getting through that, even with the support of her family and friends, raising a teenage girl while she worked two jobs. Losing Wade was Darci's greatest fear in life, one of the things that made her work so hard to establish her business, in case she ever had to go it alone.

Her imagination took over. Instead of the bare tree limbs and blue sky her eyes focused on, she saw a woman dressed in turn of the century clothes like Miss Addie's, a baby in each arm, walking down a dusty street. Train stations from old movies also came to mind, though she didn't know if people around here still traveled that way back then.

Now she had to figure out what to do. Hopefully she wouldn't look too nosy if she let the letter writer know she'd read it. She'd probably appreciate any help she could get, by the sound of it. But what could she do for Betsy's family? Although she lived in the Brown house, it wasn't like she knew anything that could help.

But, on the other hand, this was Dixon, Kentucky. Small towns have very few secrets. Like herself, most local families had been living there for generations. She knew Charlotte would be interested in this, since any gossip, even from a hundred years or so ago, would grab her attention.

As for the line in the letter about passing the note on to 'Miss Addie's people', lucky for them she just happened to know one blood relative. But what would Hattie think about the situation? The way she'd waxed nostalgic when she first came to the shop, Darci imagined she'd be very eager to meet her grandma's friend's relations, and there was a very good possibility she might know something. And obviously, she'd be able to ask around to her cousins, see if they remember their grandma talking about Betsy's husband.

Wade would give her that little grin of his, she was sure, the one that said he thought Darci just loved putting herself in the middle of stuff. At least this was a simple matter of finding a family's real last name, pretty much, where a few adults wanted to carry out their great-grandmother's dying wish, not some big crime cover-up that would get her shot at again.

She shuddered, and then shoved that thought

out of her mind.

That afternoon Darci worked on Easter wreaths and decorative baskets. Charlotte sat beside her in the workroom, putting the final touches on one the Baptist church down the street ordered to put on their front door for sunrise service that coming Sunday.

Charlotte yawned as she wired an artificial daffodil in place. She reached for a few springs of greenery as Darci finished filling her in on the letter.

"It's so weird, you know, to think that something happened here in Webster County that made that poor lady run off with two newborns. Weirder still that they're connected to our favorite ghost."

"How did she react to the news? The usual chill, or did she rattle the windows?" Charlotte winked at her cousin. "Always thought it would be cool if she tried that."

"A cold spot and Daisy chirping away. Don't know that I particularly encourage rattling windows." Darci cut her eyes at Charlotte. "So, you think I should give them a call? Thought I might invite them down, and Hattie would probably jump at the chance to meet with them. You in?"

"Hell yeah." Charlotte fluffed out a strand of wire-edged ribbon fashioned into a bow on the side of the church's wreath. "Whole thing sounds kinda like a soap opera, what with the baby daddy questions, inheritance, and the part about Betsy thinking somebody from here might be out to do her and her kids in. I wouldn't miss it."

Petal Pushers Plant Profile for Heirloom Tomatoes

Solanum lycopersicum
Annual vegetable

Some of my favorite heirloom tomatoes are Mr. Stripey, Brandywine, Mortgage Lifter, Cherokee Purple, and Black Krim.

Brief description: Heirloom tomatoes vary in color from yellow to pink, dark red to purple to nearly blackish in color, and some are actually striped. Heirlooms range from cherry size to extra-large. Most gardeners and foodies agree that these tomatoes are packed with a whole lot more flavor than your regular grocery store variety.

Trivia: Heirloom tomatoes are grown from seeds that have been passed down for many generations. Some date back a hundred years or so. Tomatoes belong to the nightshade family, which might explain why folks in colonial times thought they were poisonous.

Growing instructions: Grow heirlooms like you would regular tomatoes. Petal Pushers offers the best selection and the most varieties in the area, so stop by and pick up a few plants the next time you're in town.

Uses: Use these delicious varieties in your favorite recipes, can them, or serve sliced with any
meal.

Chapter Two

*The violets in the mountains have broken
the rocks.*
~ Tennessee Williams

Darci anxiously waited for her guests to arrive. A
pale yellow tablecloth draped the dining table
that served as the flower shop's extra work space.
She wanted everyone to have plenty of room to
take notes and lay out the papers Ellen mentioned she was going to bring, and what better
icebreaker than having snacks right in the middle of everything. Charlotte helped her set the
kitchen table, the good china creamer and sugar
bowl Darci found at the flea market last week in
the center, napkins to the side, a stack of pretty
paper plates underneath. A tray of finger sandwiches, a variety of pickles, sliced fruit and veggies, and some kind of healthy dip that didn't
look all that appetizing sat on one side. Her first
urge was to make brownies and a cheesecake,

but her goal of losing a few pounds stood in her way. Stupid diet.

A light rain tapped against the window glass. The weather had been a bit warmer the past few days, but the sky was a pale blue behind the storm clouds, promising sunshine after the drizzle dissipated. Darci figured it was a mild taste of the spring showers that would soon make it way too muddy for her to get her hands dirty with early planting.

Hoyt was on standby to wait on any costumers who came into Petal Pushers that afternoon. Paxton was out fishing with Wade and Jimbo, and Charlotte's babysitter, Ashley Rosales, was at the Villines home tending to little Cole, so that left Darci and Charlotte free for the afternoon.

Bells jingled on the shop's front door.

"Who do you think got here first?" Darci asked as she ran her fingers through her hair. "Hattie or Ellen and her bunch?"

"My money's on Ellen and them." Charlotte popped an olive in her mouth as they walked up front. "Since they have more to gain, if they figure all this out."

"Hi, y'all come on in." Darci smiled at the three in front of her. Two carried paper and folders, the other didn't know what to do with his hands. "Which one of you is Ellen?"

"Me." The brunette wiped her feet on the welcome mat, left her green umbrella on the front porch propped against the siding, and then stepped inside. "It's so nice to meet you Darci. This is my brother Shane and our cousin Trisha."

Ellen wore her brown hair in a bob and was of average height and weight. Darci guessed her to be in her early forties, a few years older than her brother. Shane stood close to six feet tall, had his sister's dark brown eyes, and dressed as he was now in a Pittsburgh Steelers jersey, it was easy to imagine him as the jock he must have been in college. Trisha had shoulder length dark auburn hair, a full figure, and pretty green eyes; Darci pegged her age to be somewhere between her cousins, probably close enough to Ellen's to have shared classes in school.

There were a few obvious family resemblances between them, most notably their quick genuine smiles.

"This is Charlotte, my cousin and right hand woman here at the flower shop." Darci gestured in her direction. "Charlotte, this is Ellen Morgan, and I guess you heard who the rest are. If you want to show everybody to the kitchen, I'll be right there."

Charlotte ushered the guests into the next room.

"Hoyt, you got a handle on everything?"

"Sure do, Boss Lady." Hoyt leaned back in the chair behind the counter, looking pleased with himself. She figured he was glad to have an easy afternoon instead of loading the van for deliveries. "Waiting on customers and answering the phone'll be a piece of cake."

"Great." Darci blared her eyes at him, but grinned. "Must you still call me that? Really." She turned and headed back to the kitchen.

"Why, yes I must, Boss Lady."

Back in the kitchen, the guests were seated around the table. Charlotte was busy putting on a fresh pot of coffee before she took the pitcher of iced sweet tea from the top shelf in the fridge and filled a glass for herself and Trisha.

Darci took a seat at the head of the table. Charlotte sat to her left, on the sink side of the kitchen, so she'd be readily available to refill glasses and such. Ellen sat to Darci's right, her brother Shane next to her. Trisha sat across from him, to Charlotte's left. The chair at the far end remained empty, waiting for Hattie to arrive and occupy the space directly across from Darci.

"How was your trip?" Darci asked to make polite conversation. She wasn't sure how long it took to drive down from Pennsylvania to western Kentucky. "Please, help yourselves to the food." She grabbed a finger sandwich so the others wouldn't be shy, and bit into her pimento cheese.

"The flight was fine." Shane crunched a gherkin in half. "Thank goodness I talked these two out of the road trip they planned. I think we would've killed each other cooped up in Ellen's Ford for eight or nine hours."

"Killjoy." Trisha's eyes danced over the glass as she sipped her sweet tea.

"We barely made it through the ride to the airport. This one won't listen to anything on the radio that came out after 1982," he said, pointing his thumb toward his cousin, "and that one only listened to country crap and hoedown music. I tried to bang my head against something to

20

drown out their taste in tunes, but the headrest was padded. The ringing in my ears was an improvement, at least."

"We can still rent a car for the trip back, if you keep acting up." Ellen gave him a look and Trisha backed her up on the threat.

Ellen's comment reminded Darci of the way Wade and his brother bantered back and forth. At least they were comfortable enough with them already to be themselves. She dipped a celery stick in the dip, made a face, since it tasted as weird as it looked, and spit it into her napkin. "Eew, this is nasty. Wait." She excused herself to toss it in the trash, removed the dip from the table and replaced it with French onion dip Paxton liked to have on hand for when his friend Jake came over in the afternoons to play video games.

"Where are y'all staying?" Charlotte asked.

"The Holiday Inn in Henderson," Ellen said. "We ate lunch at a great little sushi place just down the street from there."

The bells on the front door jingled again. Hoyt showed Hattie to the kitchen, where she joined the rest of them. Charlotte, who'd met her at Petal Pushers' New Year's Eve party four months before, made the introductions.

"It's so nice to see you again, Hattie." Darci gave her a hug. "Hope the drive up from Clarksville didn't tire you out. Where's Gene?"

"The drive was fine, and Gene's visiting some friends over in Lisman. I'm supposed to call him when we finish up, so he'll know when to come get me." Hattie took her seat, smoothing out her

21

skirt as she sat, then hooked her purse over the back of the chair.

"Here." Darci leaned across the table to hand Hattie some extra paper and a pen. "So you can take notes, if you want."

"Thank you, dear." Hattie took her seat while Charlotte poured her a cup of coffee. The group made small talk for a few more minutes before they got down to the business that brought them together.

"Ellen, would you mind catching Hattie up on the information you have?" Darci opened a spiral notebook and clicked the ink pen she'd stuck in the wire edge. "I read her your letter over the phone, but I honestly don't know if I remembered all the details you gave me."

"I do hope we can help find the answers you're looking for, but even if we don't, it's so nice for all of us to be here together." Nostalgia glowed in Hattie's eyes as she talked. "Grandma spoke so highly of Betsy. I believe Aunt Virginia went with her once when she visited your great-grandma years ago. I wish Aunt Virginia or my daddy was still with us, God rest their souls. Can I ask you a question before I forget?"

"Sure, Hattie, ask away." Ellen appeared eager to hear what she had to say, as were Shane and Trisha.

"In the letter, you referred to your great-granny as Betsy McGee, but said she assumed an alias after she left Webster County, right?"

"Yes," Trisha answered.

"How did she come about that name, McGee?"

Hattie asked. "Do you know?"

Daisy started to tweet from the next room. Hoyt whistled at her, but she kept singing away, and Darci could tell by the clatter that her parakeet was probably clutching the bars on the side of her cage, bobbing her head.

Then the cold spot hit. Darci had never told Hattie about the haunting, and wasn't about to fill her or Betsy's kin in on that fact now or at any time in the future. Bad enough it would make her sound crazy, but she couldn't imagine how Hattie would feel if she knew her beloved grandmother haunted this very house.

"We've got to get the heater fixed. Sorry about the chill, but a guy's coming to look at it next week." Darci shot a look at Charlotte.

"Um, yeah." Charlotte tried not to look like something was up, even though Darci saw the goose bumps on her forearms before Charlotte pulled her sweater sleeves back down. "Let me know if y'all get too cold and I'll turn the oven on."

"My mom and grandmother found out on Betsy's deathbed, when Great-Granny dropped the rest of the bombshell. It's stuck in my mind ever since my mother decided to tell me about it a few months ago. As a matter of fact, I had a dream about Betsy that prompted me to write that letter." Ellen cleared her throat. "Was McGee Addie's maiden name?"

Hattie nodded. Her fingers traced the horizontal figure eight of the pin she wore on her blouse, the one Darci knew was left to her by Miss Addie.

23

The same one given to Miss Addie by Betsy all those years ago, after the birth of the twins.

Trisha reached over and patted Hattie's hand. "Betsy was afraid somebody was going to come after her and the babies. She couldn't let anybody know who she was, so your grandmother told her she could use her maiden name. Weren't many McGees in the area then, they reasoned. Great-Gran said none of them would've made it, her included, if it wasn't for Addie sticking her neck out for them. Funny, she always talked about how proud she was to be a McGee, way before she told us any of this. Now it's even more significant."

"Damn shame she didn't decide to lay all this on everybody when she was in good health, or even when we had a chance to ask her about it." Shane speared an olive with a cocktail toothpick. "I mean, yeah, I think there's something to it, but my dad thinks it's just a bunch of BS brought on by the meds she was on, or just plain ole delirium."

"Grandma Addie was so proud of her family, where she came from." Hattie sat up a little straighter. "To me, it feels like Grandma pretty much adopted Betsy as her own kin, to protect her with her daddy's last name."

"Let me start at the beginning, to make sure we don't leave out anything." Ellen opened the thick binder she'd brought in with her and leafed through a few pages of handwritten notes. "You know Adelaide Brown was the midwife who delivered Betsy's babies back in 1905. My grandma

Ella and Trisha's grandma Emma. They were about three days old when Great-Granny lost her husband and fled. We're not sure how long they lived in Dixon, since she used to talk about when she was first married and living in Missouri." She pulled some paperclipped pages out of one of the folders and passed them around the table. "These are copies from the family bible. You three can each keep one. I made copies of everything we have documented so far."

"It gives Ella and Grandma's birth place as Dixon, Kentucky," Trish said as she passed the sheets from Hattie to Charlotte.

"Okay," Shane said, raising his hand. "All this grandma and great-grand talk is making my head spin, so I imagine it's confusing the heck out of the rest of you. I suggest that during these conversations, we use the ladies' actual names."

"Sounds good to me," Charlotte said. "I was already kind of confused."

Darci ran her fingers over the copies of Betsy's family bible. The age of the original document was apparent in the shading and the artfully looped cursive handwriting. The entries above the birth inscription drew her attention. Betsy's date of death was written in someone else's hand, probably one of her daughters'.

"Hey, at least you have some information about Betsy's husband. His birthday, their wedding date." Darci's finger slid over the writing. "I'd expected his original name to be scratched out, but I see she wrote L. S. McGee." She looked up at Ellen. "Did she get this bible after she moved

25

away?"

"That's what we think. Now it makes us wonder if she had time to get any of her things together before she left." Ellen locked eyes with Trisha. "If she was really running for her life and the babies', I can't imagine what she must've had to leave behind."

"Any idea what the initials stand for?" The wheels in Darci's mind were already turning, even though they'd barely scratched the surface.

"Not a clue. Mom said the only thing she remembers Gr-, I mean Betsy, referring to him as was granddaddy," Shane said. "You know, as in 'your granddaddy this and that'. And Ella and Aunt Emma said she did the same when they were growing up, only with 'your pa did so and so'."

"How did Betsy's husband die?" Hattie cast a sympathetic glance to Ellen, Shane, and Trisha. "This bible page lists his passing days after the girls were born." She looked back down at the page in her hand. "Funny that the line for final resting place isn't filled in."

"It is. We were all under the impression before that it was some kind of accident. Betsy's daughters and grandkids said she got real upset if they asked anything about what happened to him." Ellen continued, "She'd tear up and leave the room."

"Same deal about his grave." Trisha swirled the ice around her glass as she spoke. "That wouldn't get her as upset as the other, but she'd say it didn't matter where his final resting place

26

is, because Pa or Granddaddy was with Jesus, just waiting for the day we'd all be together. And honestly, I don't think any of us were curious about it, until all this came out."

They went on through the afternoon discussing the details and vital statistics known about L. S. and Betsy. They were no closer to solving this riddle, but they had a few ideas how they might go about searching for answers. Hattie and Gene were going home to Tennessee that evening, even though Darci invited them to use her guest room; she knew they were afraid they'd be putting her out. Ellen, Shane, and Trisha were going to stay in Henderson for a couple of days before they went back to Pennsylvania. Before everyone called it an evening, talk turned to when they could get together again.

They exchanged phone numbers and email addresses, Gene's since Hattie didn't fool with such things, preferring good old fashioned letters for a more personal touch in her correspondence. Darci would act as coordinator to keep everyone up on anything that turned up.

"I really appreciate you having us all down this afternoon, Darci." Ellen gathered her notes, tucked them neatly back into her binder, now a little thicker than when she'd got there. "What made you want to help us?"

"Ah, what's in it for me, huh?" Darci thought about it for a second. "I feel a connection to Miss Addie-"

Charlotte cleared her throat as a signal for Darci not to lose her mind, though she had no intention of it.

". . . since my shop is where she lived and raised her family." Darci's grin got bigger when Charlotte realized she hadn't been about to talk about the ghost that was probably listening to them right at that second. She should have re-membered what Darci told her about having no intention to ever let Hattie know her grandma haunted the place. How would any normal per-son handle information like that, that their loved one was trying to one up Casper? "Plus I'm kind of into history, and honestly, just plain nosy. I want to know what happened, why it happened, all that good stuff. No telling what kind of secret made Betsy clear out of here at a moment's no-tice, and what kind of people would want to hurt her and the babies."

"Well, we truly appreciate the hell out of any help you can give us with this." Trisha gave her a one armed hug.

"I second that." Shane stood to go. "I thought my sister had lost it when she sent that letter to Adelaide's address. Your call was so much better than the returned envelope I expected. Of course, I was disappointed I didn't get to tell her I told you so, but I'll get over it. So long as these two don't make me listen to a medley of god-awful country and eighties pop on the way back to the hotel." He faked a shiver as Trisha smacked him on the arm.

"Hattie," Ellen said. "Do you have anything of Addie's that might help? A stack of letters tied with a ribbon, a scrapbook, anything of that sort?

Did she keep records of the babies she delivered, since she was a midwife? I have no idea if that's something they would do back then."

"Not that I can think of, I'm sorry. I have our family bible that my daddy passed down to me. It used to be Walt and Addie's. She tucked little slips of paper between some of the pages, which I believe was kind of a custom in her day, but I don't think there's anything important in there. I'll check as soon as we get back home, though. You never know." Hattie paused to think. "Grandma, I mean Addie, was the type to hang onto things. Pictures the grandkids drew, church bulletins, and I know she saved old letters. Once she showed me some old love notes my grandpa wrote before they married. But you have to remember she's been gone now for better than seventy years."

"Well, I knew it was a long shot but I thought I should ask, just in case." Ellen patted Hattie's shoulder.

A cold breeze swept across the room. They'd walked toward the door and now stood in the main room. Daisy tweeted in her familiar frenzy, feathered head bobbing, her tiny little eyes pointed in Hattie's direction.

Oh, my Hattie girl, you don't have to rush off so soon. I cain't understand how you got so old when my back was turned. Seems like you still ought to be your little six-year-old self, helping me cut out sugar cookies. Time just doesn't make sense any-

29

more.

Whatever you do, take your time goin' through those boxes, like I'm a-tellin' you. You'll find every-thing you're lookin' for, you'll just have to figure a few things out before they'll make good sense.

And I expect to get a hug before you leave.

"A thought just popped into my mind!" Hattie looked excited, enlightened even.

"When we decided to sell this house, there was still some stuff left in here. My uncle was the last person to stay here, but that was just briefly, right after his wife passed away. My dad and his brother and sister got together after Grandma passed, to divvy up the furniture and household goods, but there were some old trunks up in the attic, a few old boxes down in the root cellar, and some loose odds and ends in a few of the closets. Did you find anything we forgot when you bought the place, Darci?"

"No, everything was empty," Darci answered, grateful she hadn't thrown anything in the trash that would be worth opening a vein over in hindsight. "The realtor told me the owner, well, I guess that would be you and yours, moved the last of the family belongings out before he started showing it. And I do believe I'm the only one who had a chance to walk through, since I snapped the place up."

"Good. My son wanted to haul all that stuff, what he called junk, to the dump." Hattie cut her eyes around. "I couldn't just toss those things out, so we rented a U-Haul and took everything back home. I've been meaning to go through it all, but I haven't got around to it yet. When you get to be my age, time has a habit of slipping away. I just kept thinking what a treat it would be to find some little something of Grandma's." Sentimentality made her forget the agreement they made to refer to their elders by their given names, but everyone knew who she was speaking of. "A potholder, an old shoe. Just anything Grandma or Grandpa held in their own hands."

"I know just what you mean." Trisha blew her nose. It was the first time she'd done that all afternoon, and then she dabbed at the corners of her eyes. "I have a ratty old green sweater Grandma Emma used to wear around the house. When I'm missing her the most, I put it on. Makes her feel a little closer."

Now it was Hattie who put an arm around Trisha. Shane handed her a tissue, then looked away, like men do when they're trying their damnedest not to show emotion.

"That is the strangest thing." Hattie paused by the front door. "I could almost swear I smell Grandma's perfume." She sniffed the air and smiled. "Vanilla, rose, and amber. Just like the first time I came here. "

The other guests also seemed to detect it once Hattie mentioned the scent. Darci knew it was Miss Addie.

"Smells nice." Ellen gave the air another sniff. "The only scent I ever knew Betsy to wear was lemon verbena."

Charlotte tried to hide the fact that she also smelled it. "That must be from those new candles we got a few weeks ago."

"Yeah, Hattie," Darci chimed in. "I'll send you one, if you'd like."

"Thanks, dear. That's so sweet of you." Hattie beamed, but Darci wished she hadn't been so hasty. Now she'd have to spend the evening searching for amber, rose, and vanilla scented candles online.

Gene pulled their car to the curb in front of the shop. Hattie had mentioned earlier that her husband's sciatica had been acting up, so he wouldn't be coming in. After the two hour car trip, then the long visit with his friends, he'd be ready for Hattie to drive so he could pop a Loratab and sleep on the trip home. She promised to look through any boxes in the storage building and get back to them in the off chance she found anything of use, and that she'd also call her Aunt Virginia's children, to see if they had any of Addie's mementos.

The front door didn't want to open, a phenomenon that always happened when Hattie left Petal Pushers. "I'm gonna have to hit these hinges with some WD-40." Darci yanked on the knob until she was afraid she was going to pull a muscle from the effort, and finally it opened.

Darci and Charlotte waved from the front porch after Shane walked Hattie to her car. Ellen cranked up their rental and after her brother and cousin piled in, she gave a little toot as their car pulled away. Darci could hear Cyndi Lauper's

"Girls Just Wanna Have Fun" blaring from the car stereo. In the backseat, Shane pressed his hands and forehead against the window and mouthed 'help me'.

Sweet Tea

Ingredients:
2 Family size tea bags
1 1/4 cups of sugar, or to taste
Water
A few slices of lemon and/or orange

Pour a little boiling water over the tea bags and let them steep for about five minutes.

While you wait, measure the sugar into a family size pitcher, and drop in the sliced lemon or orange. (Don't use too many slices if you're going to keep the tea overnight, since it might take on too much flavor. I don't usually use more than three.)

Squeeze the liquid out of the bags and pour the tea over the sugar and sliced fruit in the pitcher. Stir until the sugar is good and dissolved, then fill the pitcher to the top with water.

Serve in tall glasses over ice.

Chapter Three

Take thy plastic spade,
It is thy pencil; take thy seeds, thy plants,
They are thy colors.
~ William Mason

"Charlotte, it's finished!" Darci wasted no time hollering after the workman left. "They're done, so come on, let's go have a look!"

Her cousin came up front wiping her hands on her jeans. "I can't believe you didn't pass out when you wrote the check. But," she added before Darci could start to worry, "this is going to be great for business."

The weather was a pleasant sixty-two degrees so neither bothered with their jackets as they went out back. First they circled around the new greenhouse, brainstorming ideas about what to plant around the outside. A florist simply can't let any part of the landscape go undecorated by foliage and blooms.

They opened the door and stepped inside. Even nearly empty, the spacious interior put a smile on both their faces. The panels already made the inside warmer than the temperature outdoors, even without the heating and cooling system being on.

Darci stretched her arm overhead so her fingertips could skim along the new misting system while she walked the length of the building. "When Hoyt gets here this afternoon, I'll get him to haul those boxes out of the cellar. We should be able to get the tables and shelves put together before closing time, then tomorrow, we'll christen this baby with some starter pods full of seeds."

"Now aren't you glad you listened to me about having the crew install the lights and electrical stuff?" Charlotte flicked a circulation fan off and on to illustrate her point. "Considering the time you saved by not having to bring in an electrician, the cost definitely balanced out."

"Yep, you were right, which is a pretty good reason to keep you around here, huh?" Darci winked at her. "Now we just need to keep this thing as productive as possible, so I can pay it off before I get an ulcer."

That night she browsed through a catalog trying to decide which kinds of snapdragons to order. It was too late to grow them from seed, but she couldn't wait to fill the new greenhouse with flats of these, since they sold well as bedding plants and added pizazz to fresh arrangements. She circled pictures as she narrowed down her options, making sure to include heirloom varieties along with new hybrids in a rainbow of colors.

"Hey, Hon, how about you invite Donovan and Bradley over for dinner?"

"Um, okay, but what's the occasion?" Darci asked, reluctantly setting down her plant catalog. "This is the first time I remember you being interested in a dinner party. Shall we do black-tie or backyard barbecue?" These last words were said in a mock Thurston Howell the third voice, or, she guessed, she probably sounded more like Mrs. Howell.

"Ha, ha, very funny, my little Lovey." Wade grinned at her. "I'll throw some steaks on the grill, but you can wear a tie if you want."

"At least you figured out who I was imitating."

"Stetson called yesterday and gave me the go ahead to start the renovations as soon as I'm ready. I think I mentioned that Bradley is the architect."

"Oh yes, you and Donovan both have told me." Last week when she got her bangs trimmed at the Hair Dare Your 'Do Salon, Donovan Lewis practically exuded pride as he told her, again, about all the hard work Bradley had been putting in on the construction plans. Wade had only mentioned it five or six times these past few months. It said a lot when Wade was this impressed with someone's work.

"We can go over a few things after dinner. I have questions about a few of the details, some pocket doors and electrical wiring and stuff. The additions should go pretty smoothly, but when you go redoing the inner workings of a building that is well over a hundred years old, you have to be prepared for some snags here and there." Wade was quiet for a minute. Darci well knew the look on his face meant he was daydreaming about getting his hands on the project.

That's one thing the two of them had in common. Neither were what you'd call work-a-holics, but their careers were their obsessions, his working with wood and such to create beautiful homes and decor, hers everything garden and flower related.

"What exactly is he having done to Clydell Manor?" Darci asked, genuinely interested in the task that would most likely have her husband occupied from now through the end of summer, if things went according to schedule. "I imagine you're probably just itching to get your fingers on that old woodwork, the hand fitted joints and all that kind of jazz."

"Adding a pool house, kitchen modifications, knocking out a wall upstairs to begin with. With five bedrooms and it just being Stetson and his wife, they don't need all those extra rooms collecting dust." Wade leaned back in his chair and put his feet up on the coffee table. "The plan is to take out the wall connecting the master bedroom to the smallest room, the one that used to be the nursery. His wife wanted a bigger boudoir and he wanted a humongous flat screen mounted on the wall. And Mrs. Clydell inherited some of her mama's furniture she wants to make room for. An antique secretary and a few other pieces. I think she's going for a sitting area by the big window we're putting in where the old wall comes out. Oh, and a gigantic walk in closet. I almost didn't mention that detail, since I'm afraid you'll want one like it if you see it when it's done."

"Donovan did tell me about that, and he's already picked out a space in his bedroom for one just like it. The two of us are gonna gang up on you and Bradley until we each get one, so there." Darci pulled a face and stuck out her tongue. "Donovan said he nearly drooled on the blueprints for that closet. A *whole* folder of designs *just* for the closet."

"It'll take a week to put together the custom shelving. She's been watching those reality shows about rich wives out in Hollywood, which is putting some pretty weird ideas in her head. She wants a motorized shoe rack, if you can believe it?"

"I believe it, and I want one." Darci was all ears. What red-blooded American woman in her right mind wouldn't want that? And enough shoes to fill it. "I almost hate to ask, but how many pairs of shoes will it hold?"

"About-" Wade stopped himself and grinned at her. "No way in hell I'm telling you that. You and Donovan need to figure out another plan, because a closest that big, with x number of shoes, which you also wouldn't need, would be too damn big for this house or Donovan and Bradley's. Hell, the four of us together wouldn't be able to wear that many shoes in a year."

"Oh, but it would be so much fun to try." Darci

visualized herself parading around Petal Pushers in some killer red spike heels, which would make her feet ache after about ten minutes but would look so great she wouldn't even care. She could have some comfy slippers under the counter, and a collection of boots for working outside and landscaping. "How 'bout you put one in that extra space we have upstairs at Petal Pushers? That would be perfect."

"Don't think so, Hon." He tossed a pillow at her head.

Ellen came back to Petal Pushers Monday morning to fill Darci in on what all they'd managed to find out over the weekend. Shane and Trisha were still at the hotel packing.

The shop was slow, as usual for a Monday morning, so Darci pulled two chairs up to the marble top table beside the porthole window, one for herself and one for her guest. Charlotte was busy in the back, so Darci wanted to stay up front in case a customer wandered in. With pleasantries out of the way, they got down to business.

"Saturday we met with a genealogist, Mrs. James. She's familiar with Webster County and the surrounding area, but since we didn't have a last name to go by, she couldn't point us toward any leads, yet anyway." Ellen took a folder out of her tote bag and withdrew a few handwritten pages. "Here, these are for you."

"Um, I thought you just said she wasn't much help." Darci glanced over the papers in her hand.

"No help on Betsy's husband, but she had some interesting ideas concerning Betsy." Ellen positioned her copy on the table beside her.

A few words jumped out at Darci. "Oh, I see." She looked up and smiled, eager to learn more.

"After she found out we didn't know a damn thing about L. S. or his background, she focused on Betsy. Wanted to know any ethnic information we have on her, where she was born, anything at all." Ellen grinned. "She got a kick out of it when I said I called her Great-Granny, if that would help."

"What more would she need?" They giggled.

"Exactly. We knew from the family bible that her maiden name was Hicks. My mom told me Betsy mentioned not having much as she grew up, and thought she was born in Missouri. That led Mrs. James to think Betsy could be Native American."

"Yeah, Hattie remembered Miss Addie saying Betsy was Cherokee," Darci said. After their visit the other day, it crossed her mind as a little odd that Betsy's family hadn't mentioned their Cherokee heritage, but she figured it may just be something they didn't think twice about. Darci's great-grandparents were French, though it seldom came up in conversation.

"Well, it was a surprise to us." Ellen smiled. "At least now I know for sure she was right about it, and where we get our cheekbones."

"I just assumed you knew. How did the genealogist figure that out?"

"Because we think Betsy was born in Missouri in 1885," Ellen said, pointing to a paragraph on the notes. "Mrs. James explained that the surname Hicks is a common Cherokee name. I know, I know, I was ignorant enough to think Indians in the cowboy days all lived in teepees and called themselves things like Suzy Sparrow or Big Chief Purple Bear of the Fire Stick. Needless to say, Mrs. James gave me a quick lesson on Native American culture. The Cherokees were marched in the Trail of Tears in 1839, but had been living like the white settlers for at least a hundred years before that. Lived in houses, had their own government and schools, even chose white people's fashion trends of the day, though they wore tribal costumes on special occasions."

"Hey, did you know the Trail of Tears went right through here? Well, pretty darn close to here." Darci told her about the annual Pow Wow she attended last September, hosted in a park where the Cherokees had camped during the forced march.

Ellen sat in thought for a minute. "Most of the Cherokee reservations were in Oklahoma, not far from Missouri where Betsy was born. When people left the rez, it was common for them to settle in the bordering states. Wish I'd've known growing up. I think it's pretty cool."

Ellen held up another paper she'd brought with her. "Mrs. James told me to go back and look at middle names from Betsy's kids and grandkids. Some people used family surnames as first and middle ones, so maybe somebody got named after L. S. So far, that's turned up a big fat nothing."

"You might want to send us a list of all those names," Darci suggested. "One set of eyes might pick up on something another misses."

"Sure thing. Trisha's mom is working on it as we speak. Problem is they all sound like ordinary names, Sally Sue and Mary Jane and William Paul. No secret messages on any of those birth certificates." Ellen look a little like she hated to admit what was about to come out of her mouth. "To speed things along a little, I hired Mrs. James to research Betsy's husband. I'm kind of in over my head right now, but she was talking about record searches, sifting through genealogy messsage forums, looking up marriage certificates, deeds. My damn head started to spin, so I found out what her fee was, put a limit on what we had to spend, and asked her to jump on it."

"Great idea. When does she think she'll know something?" Darci asked.

"She has a few other trees she's already climbing, but said she'd clear a day at the end of next week and see what she can come up with." Ellen sounded disappointed at the delay, but hopeful about the possibilities.

"Okay, keep me posted on every little thing she digs up. I love a good mystery and can't wait to see what you find out about this one. No telling what you'll dig up."

"I promise. And you do the same. Even if you think something you stumble across is insignificant." Ellen opened her folder and traded the paper in her hand for another one, and its Xeroxed twin, which she handed to Darci. "Here's your copy of my notes from our other meeting. This one was with Dave Pearson, the historian who specializes in western Kentucky."

"I'm surprised anybody would specialize in these small towns when they could study Louisville, or the places Davy Crockett went through. Then again, maybe there's interesting stuff around here I haven't thought of. Like how people don't go see the sights in their own back yard, like a Frenchman who never visits the Eiffel Tower, or a New Yorker who doesn't go to the Statue of Liberty. Well, just like I never knew about the Pow Wow in Hopkinsville until my son told me about it."

"Well Dave seemed to know his stuff, and he's pretty enthused about the area." Ellen rolled her eyes. "Some of the info he rattled off was pretty boring. I almost fell asleep once, but Shane kicked me under the table. Once would have done it, but he made sure I had two bruises on my shin, and him sitting there with a grin on his stupid face. But, I digress."

"Digress away, it's all fascinating to me." Darci meant it. As an only child, she'd always felt like she'd missed out on the fun sibling rivalry she saw when she'd stayed over at her friends' houses as a kid. Well, she wasn't jealous of Charlotte's brother, since he grossed them out with boogers and fake blood; she cringed just thinking about her cousin Chet.

"With Betsy being too afraid to mention her husband's real name even in the relative safety of the pages of the family bible, that alone, in his opinion, leads credence to the things she spoke of on her deathbed." Ellen scanned her finger down her copy of notes. "She believed someone from her late husband's family was after her and the twins, and from what she said, she feared for their lives."

Hoyt walked through the back door, right on time, as usual. He didn't seem to notice them, and probably figured Darci was back in the work room since she wasn't behind the counter. His head bobbed in time to the music streaming through his earbuds, which seldom left his ears. He apparently thought he was all by his lonesome, which prompted him to dance to his tunes.

Darci covered her mouth to stifle her laughter, and made the 'shhh' sign to Ellen, who watched with her mouth gaping open. Darci stood and motioned for Ellen to join her in sneaking up behind Hoyt while his back was still turned to them. He could spin around any second and what fun would that be, if she wasn't standing right there to surprise him?

Hoyt struck a pose with his hand extended, his legs moving like a bowlegged cowboy stomping fire ants.

Right then Darci signaled Ellen to join in. They stepped to either side of Hoyt, Gangnam Style, pretending not to look at his horrified expression.

"Aw, come on, Boss Lady!" Hoyt jerked the buds out of his ears. "That's not cool, sneaking up on a guy like that."

"Also not cool calling me Boss Lady," Darci said through laughter induced tears. "That was priceless. I didn't have you pegged as a Psy fan, but you sure have his moves down." She winked at Ellen and danced a few more steps. "Gangnam Style!"

They sat back down after Hoyt stomped outside, then pulled themselves together and got back to their notes.

"Dave, the historian, said countless families have lost touch with their Native American roots because people hid it up through the first half of the twentieth century." Ellen leaned back in her chair. "Even in the nineteen hundreds, until the fifties I think he said, there were schools out west where the government made the Native American parents of some tribes send their kids. Can you imagine having absolutely no choice where your own children went or what kind of crap they were being taught? To say they weren't treated well is a gross understatement."

"I had no idea." Darci was blown away.

They sat in silence for a few minutes, each in their own thoughts, until their minds went back to the matter at hand.

"Did the historian have any idea what could've happened to L. S.?" Darci asked. "Can he think of any reason why people would want to hurt Betsy and the babies? Was anything weird going on in the area then? Mother-in-law jokes aside, I can't imagine why a man's family would be driven to threaten a widow and two newborns."

"All he could do was speculate like we're doing."

"So right now, our best shot is hoping the genealogist can find a name through a marriage license or something. I really hate to ask, because if the answer is no you're gonna want to strangle me," Darci said, "but do you have any idea where they were married?"

"Nope, but I won't smack you." Ellen smiled at her new friend and confidant. "We checked the Webster County records on the internet and found nothing for Betsy Hicks. Same thing with Hopkins and Henderson counties. Oh yeah, here's another bit of joy I forgot to mention. Old names, spellings, nicknames." Ellen rolled her eyes. "Betsy could be Great-Grandma's given name, or short for Elizabeth. And there are a few different spellings for Hicks, one with an 'x', plus the possibility that whatever made her run after her husband died might also have made her give a different maiden name. Old Dave said she probably wouldn't have dared tell anyone in 1904 that she was a Cherokee. Remember the Battle of Wounded Knee, where the Sioux were massacred by US soldiers?" Darci nodded. "That happened in 1890."

A customer walked in, so Darci excused herself for a few minutes to wait on the lady who needed to buy some daffodil bulbs, and wanted instructions on how to get them to bloom the next month. Darci explained that the ideal way to go about that was to set all spring bulbs in fall or early winter. The lady walked out with a Petal

Pushers bag full of assorted bulbs, a large rectangular pot under her arm, and the knowledge of how to put the bulbs in the freezer for a few days before she tried to 'force' them indoors.

Ellen had to leave to catch her flight, so they finished their discussion as Darci walked her to the door.

"The genealogist knows where all the records and search engines are, so with my fee fueling her along, let's keep our fingers crossed that she finds a Betsy marrying some guy in 1904 with the initials L. S. Or least a first name that starts with 'L'."

"Where do you want me to start poking around?" Darci asked. "Any records from Webster County you want me to search, historical facts to look up, just name it."

"You've already introduced us to Hattie, opened your shop to us, and got us organized. We can't thank you enough," Ellen said. "I have to admit, I don't know if I'd be able to volunteer my time to help a bunch of strangers figure out something like this, something that in the scheme of the world just isn't very important, except to my family, that is."

"No thanks necessary." Darci meant it from the bottom of her heart. "Living in Miss Addie's house makes me feel connected, and Hattie's my friend, and you saw how she perked up at the chance to reconnect with her grandma's bestie's family."

"Well, just remember how very appreciated you are," Ellen reiterated. "Don't let us take up any more time than you're willing to give, and only while you're enjoying it. When we get back around to the banging our head against the wall in frustration stage, you'll see what I mean."

Darci and Charlotte drove down the road in the delivery van. Some lucky little girl was about to receive a hundred and fifty pink and yellow balloons for her big birthday party. A meadow full of grazing horses came into sight as they crested a hill. The van slowed down when they passed a large barn, one now very familiar to both women. A new sign drew Darci's attention.

"Well, I for one am thrilled to death they finally decided to change the name." Darci gripped the wheel a little tighter, her thumbs snapping the edges of the leather steering wheel cover.

"Don't you ever let me hear you use the word death and yourself in the same sentence." Charlotte was serious, using a tone of irritation and concern Darci hadn't heard since last September. "So not funny, especially considering one of the dudes who owned that place. May his ass rot in jail."

"Sorry, you're right. Bad pun, if that would even qualify as one." Darci cleared her throat. The fingers of one hand found their way to the little scar on her forehead, which she rubbed a few seconds before she realized what she was doing. Without thinking about it, she'd nearly come to a stop in the middle of the road in front of the business now renamed Maldonado Stables. She pushed on the gas petal. "Nice to see the 'N' off that sign."

"I second that." Charlotte nodded, staring down the road in front of them.

Max had told her that Paula Maldonado sued Roy Nolan civilly, after he was convicted of murder and sentenced to life in the federal penitentiary. She and her family won full ownership of the stables, plus his car, which they promptly sold. He thought she divvied up the cash between her grandchildren, but wasn't sure about that detail. Max also knew she could easily have gotten the deed to his house, the only thing Roy hadn't lost in his losing gambling streak, mainly because his mother's name was also on the lease. Nolan had hidden a lot of things from his mother.

Paula refused to go after the deed for just that reason, bless her heart. Roy would never experience a minute of freedom again, something he well deserved for killing her husband and Nolan's business partner, Cyril Maldonado, not to mention the attempted murder Darci could still barely stand to think about without breaking out in a cold sweat. He'd never have use for that house again, but his poor mother had Paula's full sympathy. What could be worse than knowing your only child was behind bars forever, taking any possibility of grandchildren with him. Paula told the lawyer she wasn't about to touch it, and asked him to convince poor Teresa Nolan to sell the damned place and buy something nice for herself.

The same criminal had set out to destroy both of their lives. Thankfully, Darci and her family were still intact, healthy, and very much alive.

"I hope they got rid of every last trace of that bastard. Cyril was a saint, to hear Ashley talk about him. He certainly didn't deserve to die that way, poisoned like a packrat," Charlotte said.

"Like a mole, actually." Darci put her hand over her mouth when she heard her own words. She'd thought them, but hadn't intended to speak them.

Charlotte shot her with a narrow-eyed glare, then caved. "Okay, I get it. Joking about things makes you feel better when the stress is on. Want to talk about it?"

Her fingers traced her scar again. "Not really, but thanks for always being here for me when I need you, whether I'm getting on your nerves or not. Which I sometimes really, really like to do." She winked at her cousin slash best friend. "You make the funniest faces."

Darci drove in silence for the next few minutes, her mind playing back the scene in her life she wished she could forget, but that she didn't want to discuss right now. Last fall, she took it on herself to go to Roy's mother's home to get samples of the *Ricinus communicus*, better known around western Kentucky as mole beans or castor plants. She'd stumbled across information that led her to rightfully believe Roy used the plant to poison Cyril. Bad thing was, Roy called his mom right as she was leaving, and she told him all about their visit.

The next morning, Darci had squatted out on the side yard at Petal Pushers, picking up a mess of overturned flower pots. Thanks to Miss Addie using her ghostly powers to ring the bells on the front door, Darci had moved at the same second Roy squeezed off a bullet aimed at her head. The scar was from the flower pot he hit instead, which sent fragments of terracotta shrapnel into the right side of Darci's head and arm.

She shivered now, just thinking about how Max came in and found her huddled under the counter. She didn't even remember Hoyt crawling out to answer the door, which she'd locked after she scrambled inside.

With a shake of her head, she pushed away all thoughts of the shooting and focused on more pleasant things. She remembered something Charlotte said a year ago and grinned.

"Hey, why don't you suck the helium out of one of those balloons and say something funny."

Charlotte took her up on it. Darci had never heard such pornographic phrases spoken in a cartoon character's high pitched squeaky voice. She nearly wet herself before they pulled into the birthday girl's driveway, rain dotting the windshield.

"What?" Wade sat up in bed, then reached for the lamp on the nightstand.

"What time is it?" Darci's mind instantly locked on the worst case scenario of why their ringing phone woke them up in the wee hours of the night.

"Three forty-two." Wade rubbed his eyes as he picked up the receiver. "Hello?"

Darci wrung her hands and fidgeted with the hem on the top of the sheet as she watched her husband's expression change from sleepy to bad news.

After a few quick questions about when and how, Wade said, "We'll be right there. Thanks for calling."

"Oh my God, who died?" Darci ticked off her list of loved ones in her mind before he had a chance to answer. Wade and Paxton were safe here with her. Grandma Odette had sounded fine when they spoke on the phone last Tuesday, but she was pushing eighty. Her mom had high blood pressure, Max had a minor heart attack about eight years ago, and what about Baby Cole? Wasn't sudden infant death syndrome a threat until after they reached a year old? She bit her lip and noticed she was hyperventilating. "What's wrong?"

'Fire' was the only word that registered before Darci grabbed her slippers and ran to the door.

Petal Pushers Plant Profile for Wandering Jew

Tradescantia zebrina, Zebrina Pendula
House plant

Wandering Jews are also called inch plant, spiderwort, and Moses-in-the-cradle.

Brief description: They have one to three inch long leaves variegated with striking purple and silvery green stripes, with purple undersides. *Tradescantia* come in many varieties.

Trivia: This is one of the easiest plants to propagate, a favorite of thrifty people who like a little more bang for their buck. Simply put cuttings, or pieces your cat or dog tears off when you're not looking, in a glass of water on your window sill. Add a little water every few days, and you'll soon notice new little white roots. Keep in the water about another week or so, then pot the new plants.

Growing instructions: Very easy to care for. These flourish in full sun to partial shade. Water when the soil is dry to the touch, and pull off any dead leaves. Pinch back new growth every now and then for a fuller, bushier plant.

Uses: These make beautiful hanging baskets and help filter toxins from the air.

Chapter Four

*For myself I hold no preference among flowers,
so long as they are wild, free, spontaneous.
Bricks to all greenhouses!
Black thumb and cutworm to the potted plant!*
~ Edward Abbey

As Wade pulled to a stop in front of Petal Pushers, Darci saw smoke billow up from behind the building. He grabbed her wrist to keep her from jumping out before he had a chance to turn off the windshield wipers and put the car in park.

"Everything's gonna be alright, Hon. Nobody got hurt, and the fire department has everything under control." He patted her hand. "It'll be okay."

Darci had been quiet during the short ride from her home to her flower shop. She tied the sash on her bathrobe, which Wade had tossed to her on the way to the front door, thank goodness, or else she'd be dressed only in her nightgown and slippers. She wiped a tear from her cheek, then turned to her sleeping son in the backseat. Wade had carried him to the car with a blanket wrapped around him, but Darci figured he'd wake up any minute now, with all the commotion going on. She gently shook him by the shoulder until his lids opened.

"Paxton, pumpkin, I want you to stay in the car."

"What's going on?" He sat up and rubbed his eyes.

"The storm caused some damage at the shop. Your Dad and I are fixing to go take a look."

"Hey! I'm want to-"

"Pax, you keep your butt parked in your seat. Or else," Wade gave his son a stern glance as he put the keys in his pocket.

"But-"

"You stay put or you'll be too grounded to go to Jake's camp out this weekend. You got me?"

"Yes sir," Paxton said, knowing better than to backtalk. "Can you let the window down a few inches so I can talk to the firemen, in case one needs to ask me something, you know, since I help out in the shop?"

"Okay, but you better not set one foot outside, and don't open your door either." Wade cracked the window and walked around to open Darci's door. She sat staring at the smoke and flashing lights, feeling like a lost little girl. Her need to confront the damage was overruled by her fear, fear that this could be the catastrophe that would ruin the business she'd worked so hard for. She took a deep breath, squeezed Wade's hand, and trudged to the back yard.

She felt something wet on her feet and looked down. Her slippers were a filthy mess, coated in mud. A loud thunder clap startled her, and she flinched as a lightning flash lit up the night sky. At least the rain had slowed to a weak drizzle. Not that she gave a damn right now. The smell of smoke and melted building material made bile rise in her throat, but she swallowed hard and kept moving.

On the ride over, Wade had filled her in about what he'd been told on the phone. The storm—whether the wind or lightning were to blame, no one knew yet—knocked a huge limb out of an oak tree in the back yard. It had fallen on one of the greenhouses and then caught fire, due either to lightning or from coming in contact with electrical wiring. Neighbors called the fire department in time to put out the flames before they spread to the shop, though there was some damage, mainly breakage in the panels of the other greenhouse.

Darci rounded the corner and groaned. A log with a diameter the size of an oven lay diagonally over the squashed remains of her brand spanking new greenhouse. A smaller branch connected to one end had knocked out a glass panel and a few Plexiglas sections from the old greenhouse, but that was minor. The new one was a total loss. The parts of the frame not broken were bent beyond fixing. Smoke rose around the fallen tree limb, which reminded Darci of a giant loaf of

French bread that caught fire in a basket.

One of the firemen approached and spoke to them, more or less reiterating what Wade had been told on the phone. After retelling the particulars, he patted Darci on the back. "Don't worry, little lady. Your insurance should have that building replaced in a couple of weeks."

Darci's ears tingled as everything spun around her. "Excuse me for a minute."

She staggered to the left a few steps and puked her guts out.

Darci got to Petal Pushers an hour before the shop opened the next morning. She'd hardly slept at all. Wade had practically pounded the fact that things were *not* that bad into her head. Part of her wanted to believe him, but she couldn't get the image of that ruined building out of her mind.

When they'd arrived back at their house at close to five a.m., right after they put Paxton to bed, Wade tried to make her feel better. "Hon, remember what Merle said about the insurance. They'll send an adjuster out and you shouldn't have any problem getting another greenhouse set up in a few weeks."

"No, they won't." Darci lost it. She covered her face with her hands and sobbed her heart out.

Wade handed her some tissues while he waited for her to pull herself together. When she finally came up for air and blew her nose, he asked why she was so worried about the insurance. He knew she had a policy on Petal Pushers with a deductible that wasn't too high.

"Because . . ." Darci fidgeted with her soggy Kleenex and shook her head. "I'll show you." She walked to the table in their entranceway and returned with some papers held together with a staple. She handed them to Wade, shook her head, and stared at the floor.

"What's all this?" He flipped through the papers, then cleared his throat. "Oh no. Please tell me these are just copies?"

"Nope. That's the policy I was going to take by tomorrow afternoon. See, I had it all filled out, but I couldn't make up my mind about changing the deductible. Sally from the insurance agency explained that if I paid a little more on the policy each month, I could lower the deductible. Sounded like a good idea, but you know me, I had to take my sweet time thinking about it. Who knew that damn tree was gonna fall apart and crush the thing to pieces? What are the chances of that?"

"It'll still be okay." Wade pulled Darci to his chest and she buried her face in his t-shirt.

"But I screwed up. I didn't add the new building to the policy, so I'm totally screwed. The best I can hope for from insurance is a bag of grass seed to fix the scorched spots in the yard around my flattened greenhouse. Oh, and I paid Hoyt an hour and a half of overtime to stay and help me put together the new tables and shelves. If they're not flat, I'm sure they melted." She'd wiped her eyes and blew her nose again. "Total loss."

61

Now Darci stood in the early morning dew staring at her very expensive squashed greenhouse, the charred tree still weighing it down like a ginormous blackened Lincoln Log. Another chunk of Plexiglas fell to the ground when a breeze shook the branches overhead.

She'd sent a text to Charlotte before she went to bed, so she'd read it that morning and not be surprised when she got to work. Hoyt should've got the one she sent him as she drank coffee watching the sun rise. Right now, she just wanted to be alone with her thoughts, and what was left of her ruined addition, to mull over her options.

When Charlotte arrived an hour later, she found Darci seated at the desk working on a list of ideas. She walked to the widow to look out at the charred melted mess in the back.

"Damn, Darce, this sucks." Charlotte gaped at the catastrophe. "But hey, things could always be worse. Everyone's okay, the shop itself didn't get any damage, and maybe the insurance company will cut you a check for even more than-"

"No insurance." Darci fidgeted with the pen in her hand. "That was on my to-do list for this morning, turning in the policy, changing things to lower the deductible. Lot of good that does now." She slammed her Papermate on the counter and turned to feed the parakeet.

"Shit. I almost hate to ask, but about how much does this set you back?"

"The price of a small car. I borrowed against the equity in the shop, as a separate loan, and planned to pay it back in less than two years with the extra moolah I thought we were gonna make. Double payments from the profit, like I do on the mortgage. Sure is going to be fun making that payment for something I don't even have anymore."

"Okay, that sucks even worse." Charlotte walked behind the counter and gave her cousin a hug, which nearly made Darci spill the birdseed. "So, what's the plan? How are we gonna fix it, and what do you need me to do?"

Darci changed Daisy's water before she went over her list of options with Charlotte, eager for input.

"First, I'll get the insurance agent over here to look at the other greenhouse, the one that's covered, and beg them for a settlement to fix the thing ASAP. As for the new one, the first option would be to bulldoze the mess out of my site and chalk this whole experience up as a hopeless disaster."

"Hey, just an idea, but when you call to order the new panels, could you ask if they cover new structures until they're added to the customer's policy, like when you buy a new car?" Charlotte took a seat beside Darci behind the counter.

"Won't work, but I'll run it past them anyway. I asked Wade about that last night." Darci grinned at her cousin, thinking it was funny that they still thought so much alike. Then she reached in a drawer for some Tylenol. "My head is killing me, what with being up all night after watching the firemen hose down my latest endeavor."

"Come on, this is just a small setback, and I know you'll find a way to flip this to your advantage." Charlotte looked out the window at the charred mess out back and winced. "Or at least break even. Everything happens for a reason, you know. Now what's next on that list?"

"Buying another greenhouse, and all the stuff that goes inside it." Darci tossed the pills into her mouth, washed them down with coffee, then fidgeted with the stapler. Tiny metal dashes soon littered the counter. "After we rob a bank to pay for it."

"I've still got my Bonnie costume from last Halloween." Charlotte held her fingers like guns, but her joke didn't even raise a smile from Darci. "Was there enough equity to add the cost of the second one to your mortgage? If it doesn't raise the payment too high?"

"Probably not, plus I don't want to add years to paying off the shop. Considering how well it's going so far, I don't think Mel over at the bank would jump at the idea." Darci shook her head, yawned, then lightly banged her head against the desk, hoping to either jar a good idea loose or work up the nerve to knock herself out.

Charlotte took control of the situation and interrupted Darci's little pity party. "Tell you what," she said, standing up and rolling Darci's chair back so she'd have no choice but to sit up. "I'm going to run the shop while you take yourself upstairs for a nap. You're exhausted, and sitting here worrying yourself sick isn't doing any good." She guided her toward the stairway. "We'll brain-

64

storm ideas for the money you need after you wake up."

"I can work through it," Darci said, trying to stand still. Her cousin pulled her arm like she was leading a toddler to a booster shot. "There's a stack of orders for the Baxter funeral, and I need to put those new wreaths up on the website-"

"No way, Darce." Charlotte continued to drag her through the shop. "Be a good girl and I'll have some Krispy Kremes waiting when you get up, but not a minute before noon, or I'll eat 'em all myself. Don't start up about your on-again off-again diet either, 'cuz everybody knows nothing's better for stress than chocolate and pastry."

Darci tucked herself into the daybed upstairs. Sleeplessness always made her overly sentimental, so no surprise when tears hit the pillow as she thought about how lucky she was to have Charlotte looking out for her. It felt good to be babied for a change. As her eyelids fluttered to a close, she tried to blot out the image of the smoking tree trunk by visualizing herself sitting down to a plate full of assorted donuts.

After skipping lunch to dive into three gooey chocolate covered Krispy Kremes, Darci felt a little better. The sleep helped almost as much as the donuts, and that last cup of coffee put her in the right frame of mind to think. She stood gazing out the porthole window, glad she couldn't see the shattered greenhouses from there, and tried to come up with a sensible fail-proof way to raise nearly ten grand.

"Come up with anything yet?" Charlotte asked as she placed three freshly potted plants on the rack by the back door for Hoyt to deliver to the funeral home.

"Nope. Unless you'd let me pimp you out to pole dance over at Babes-A-Rama."

"Only if you're up there with me," Charlotte shot back, doing the shimmy. "Jimbo loves it when I-"

"No, please," Darci said, grinning as she struck the talk to the hand pose. "Too much info."

"Glad you feel up to joking around. You're much more fun this way." Charlotte headed back toward the workroom. "When Hoyt comes in, have him check with me before he loads the van. I should have a couple more swags done by then."

Left to her thoughts, she focused on raising cash. Borrowing from family or friends was on her list of big no-nos, totally out of the question. She was now stuck with a sizable bank payment to make in addition to Petal Pushers' mortgage, plus not enough equity left for an additional greenhouse loan. Her frugality left little room to cut back anything in the budget, either for business or in her household.

If she could just get two greenhouses running in the next week or so, she could double what she'd made from selling slips last spring.

Adding the expense to the mortgage would raise the minimum payment, if they didn't laugh her out of the bank, plus add extra months she'd be paying interest. She wrote LAST RESORT beside that idea as she added it to her pissy little list. The next page had only a header of 'How to Pay All This Off'. With a grin, she jotted down 'Set up stripper pole for Charlotte on front porch'.

The mosaic clock on the wall drew her attention, so she paused to run her fingers over shards of antique Belleek china embedded in the edges. Hattie's voice rang through her memory from the time she'd quoted Miss Addie: 'If this piece of china could cross the Atlantic Ocean in one piece, surely to goodness I can make it through whatever small crisis comes into my life.'

Shame she didn't have money mounted to the wall with a sign that said 'Break glass for cash in case of emergency'.

"Emergency money," Darci whispered, then bent to take something out of her purse. She bit her lip as she paced the length of the room, working the small plastic card with her fingers as she walked. She halted in the middle of the room, then took a step toward the phone, but jerked her hand back before she touched the receiver. "No, I just don't know," she said out loud, then paced some more.

After a few minutes of wallowing in indecisiveness, she marched to the office chair and grabbed the mouse with a mission in mind. Double-checking the numbers from the card she plunked down on the desk in front of her, her fingers banged on her keyboard. She held her breath, hit enter, and covered her eyes. When she finally peeled her hand off her eyelashes, her heart started to race. "This could work," she mumbled, typing in more information.

"Let's do this," she said to Daisy, then swiveled her chair around before she hollered for Charlotte.

"What's up, Darce?" Charlotte came in wiping her hands on her work apron. "You sound kind of worked up."

"Believe it or not, I made a decision. Come here and sit down." Darci slid the other chair out for her.

"Okay, so what's the deal with that?" As soon as Charlotte's butt hit the seat, she raised an eyebrow at the credit card Darci had plopped in front of her and was still tapping with her fidgety index finger. "Want me to order some take out?"

"Nope, well, maybe later. Right now, I need you to sit there while I make a call, and do not let me hang up without putting in the order for our replacement greenhouse. Pinch me if you need to, or hold this up in my face if I try to weasel out." Darci handed Charlotte the loan papers from the bank that she'd signed just a few weeks before.

"Sure thing, as soon as you tell me what I'm forcing you to do. Then I'll break out the thumbscrews."

"Wade and me have this account, but keep a zero balance on it. Originally we used it build up our credit, and after a while we set it aside for emergencies. A few years ago we had to put Christmas gifts on it, and Wade used it to replace a few tools, but that was a while back too. We always paid the balance off in two months, you know how frugal I am." Darci fidgeted with the phone cord. "Anyway, I just looked at the available credit, and we have enough to replace that mess out back. What do you think?"

"That's your call, but it sounds like a good idea. I'm guessing you've checked what the minimum payment will be?"

"Yep, and you know I'll pay back as much as we're able each month until I wipe the debt out. Thing is, we have to spend money to make money in this circumstance, since I have to pay off the credit bill, the equity loan I took out, and the mortgage." Darci cupped her hands over her mouth and took a few deep breaths, trying to stop hyperventilating. "Tell me I'm doing the right thing."

"You're doing the right thing," Charlotte said, grinning, "which I think you know. Now get to dialing before you change your mind."

"Okay." Darci popped her knuckles one finger at a time before she picked up the phone. With the receiver balanced between her ear and shoulder, she angled the credit card for easy reference, reached for a pen, and scooted a notepad in front of her. "Oh, just a minute," she said, turning to the filing cabinet to pluck off the magnet with Ross Whitfield's number on it. After carefully placing that beside the phone, she glanced back at Charlotte for moral support.

"I think you're all set, unless you think you ought to paint your toenails first." Charlotte gave her a stern but encouraging nod and held up the bank payment book. "Get to dialing."

Darci stuttered a little when Ross picked up, but then got straight to business. He expressed his condolences for the storm damage, and as expected, said he was sorry insurance on his end wouldn't cover it. After a full minute of dead silence while Darci squirmed in her chair, Charlotte tapped the credit card loud enough for the thumps to echo through the store.

"Um, I guess I need to get a replacement greenhouse set up, just like the other one, with the same extras. . . .Yep, everything inside is flat as a very expensive pancake." Charlotte patted her arm as Darci and Ross discussed how soon he could get to it.

Charlotte watched her write out the details and winced as she jotted down prices, even though she already had a good idea of what the project would cost. Darci recited numbers from her emergency credit card for the deposit. Something made her smile real big right before she ended the call.

"He said he felt so bad for us, he's cutting us a deal on the extras. The tables, shelves, and all that." She drew a line through those expenses and replaced the total with a lower number. "Ross is giving those to us at his cost. Said he couldn't jiggle the numbers any on the greenhouse, but he promised to light a fire under his crew so they'll get the whole shebang up for us, wiring and all, in three business days instead of the week it took last time. That'll save on labor."

"See, that wasn't so hard. I can come in and

help you off the clock with whatever scheme you come up with, since I know you're hell bent on paying it all off ASAP. And don't forget." Charlotte slung her leg over the chair arm as she laid back seductively, doing a nearly upside down shimmy as she spun around. "Babes-A-Rama is always hiring."

"You're gonna fall off and land on your head." Darci started to comment about her being so flexible but decide against it, knowing Charlotte would say something so raunchy it might permanently warp her mind.

Ellen called Petal Pushers one afternoon when Darci had her hands in a pile of potting soil, up to her elbows transplanting some of the heirloom tomato seedlings into slightly larger pots. Charlotte told her Darci'd call back that afternoon, as soon as she had a chance.

"Hi Ellen, you rang," Darci said into the phone after she had all her little seedlings situated in the rebuilt greenhouse. She'd returned the call right after she scrubbed her arms up to the elbows, and after a nice lunch of homemade vegetable soup she'd whipped up the past weekend to keep on hand for meals at the shop. It wasn't like she could afford to order take out. "What's up?"

"Just wanted to check in." Something in Ellen's voice suggested she had interesting news. "Have you heard anything from Hattie? I'm dying to know if she's had a chance to go through those boxes and trunks. I hope she finds some treasure there, even if it doesn't give us any leads." Darci could tell she meant it.

"She called last weekend to see if you'd came up with anything. And no, she hasn't had a chance to go through those boxes, but she's itching to." Darci chuckled a little bit. "I feel for poor Gene. I bet she's about to aggravate him to death to help her, but she said his sciatica is bothering him. Some of her grandkids are supposed to go down to visit, and she promised not to feed 'em until they dust off a couple boxes and bring them into the porch."

"I bet she means it, too," said Ellen.

"So, don't keep me in suspense. Did y'all find any leads?" Darci fidgeted with the phone cord, winding it around her finger, then straightening out the curly spiral.

"Actually, I just emailed you a document Mrs. James sent me this morning."

"Great, I'll pull it up. I'm sitting at the front counter, so just let me wake up the PC." Darci typed in her email password, then clicked the little envelope beside Ellen's name. "'Kay, I'm looking at it. Dang, that's one long list of names."

"Yep, that's what I said. Mrs. James did an extensive search of marriage records, and these are the ones that listed the bride as any variation of Betsy Hicks." Ellen took a deep breath Darci heard through the receiver. "Unfortunately, none of the perspective grooms are listed as L. S. anything. Lots of first names starting with 'L's and last names starting with 'S', and then we have a bunch without 'L's or 'S's, but the right bride. These are just the ones she found for 1904, and it's a possibility they weren't even married."

"It's highly doubtful you're an illegitimate great-grandkid. Even though Betsy gave birth over a hundred years ago, somebody would've made a note of that. I almost wish that was the case." Darci, always afraid of tasting her foot in her mouth, hoped she hadn't just unintentionally offended her new friend. "You know, so we could figure it out easier."

"I know, Darci," Ellen said. "We're friends here, no need to pussyfoot."

"Well hey, this is a great place to start." Darci was genuinely hopeful as she scanned down the looooong list on the computer monitor. She clicked the mouse—after she brushed a small pile of leaves off of it. She'd have to tell Paxton not to goof around at her desk—then listened to the printer hum into action. "I'm printing it out as we speak, and me and Charlotte can go over it to-morrow. Who am I kiddin', you know I'll be all over this tonight like stink on poo, but Charlotte can help tomorrow when she comes in. We'll highlight any surnames common in Webster County. She come up with anything else?"

"No, just the list, and she reached the end of the payment we agreed on. I told her to go ahead and dig around another ten hours, to see if she could find out more." Ellen didn't sound any more eager to have an added expense than Darci would have. Friends in frugality, Darci thought. "So, we'll continue to keep fingers and toes crossed for a few weeks, which is when she'll be able to look into it. Probably won't do a lot for what we're working on, but I'd like to know. I still can't understand why Great-Grandma Betsy kept a secret like this for so long."

After she got off the telephone, Darci chose a yellow highlighter from the pencil holder on her desk. She couldn't help it, she had to make a first pass over that list. She was supposed to vacuum the shop before closing and do the weekly cleaning, but hell, she owned the joint and Hoyt was looking kind of bored out back, picking up the last of the sticks that blew down in last week's storm. She tapped on the window and motioned for him to come in so she could ask him if he'd mind using the vacuum and dust rag. "Leave the bathroom. I'll get that tomorrow. Paxton and Jake have been hanging out here a lot and I wouldn't wish cleaning up the toilet they used on anybody."

"Sure thing, Boss Lady." Hoyt pushed a button on his iPod, then shoved it back in his pocket, not thinking about what he'd just said.

"Boss Lady feels a song comin' on. Wait for it." Darci stood, arms extended like she was getting a divine calling. She shot a psycho grin right at Hoyt. "Uh-oh! Here it is. Gangnam Style!"

"Come on, give it a rest, please. It slipped, I promise." Hoyt was still embarrassed about dancing in front of her and Ellen, a fact Darci used against him each time he called her Boss Lady, his favorite term of endearment, made even dearer to him when he saw that it aggravated the piss out of her. She knew he meant it in fun, this college boy who loved to pick on people. She just didn't see herself as a Boss Lady.

With Hoyt manning the sweeper, Darci sat back with her list and highlighter. A quick glance through the grooms' last names prompted her to hit it with a streak of yellow. A folder on the edge of the desk held all the notes she had on Betsy and company. With the sheets spread in front of her, she glanced over the facts, then read over each name in the bride and groom columns.

By the time Hoyt finished vacuuming, she had to stop to take a Tylenol. Nothing jumped out at her, but at least now she had a good familiarity with all the possible Betsy Hickses and their suitors from a century ago. She put the papers in her folder, glad to have something to help take her mind off her financial problems for a while.

Petal Pushers Plant Profile for Irish Moss

Sagina Subulata
Perennial

Irish moss is also called Scotch moss and pearlwort.

Brief description: This lush groundcover grows one to two inches tall. Small white flowers bloom from late spring into mid-summer.

Trivia: It's not a true moss, but is named for the lush grassy moss-like mounds. Walking on this groundcover doesn't hurt it one bit.

Growing instructions: Buy as bedding plants or they're easy to grow from seed. Set in full sun to partial shade.

Uses: Irish moss is the perfect thing to plant around flagstones, in rock gardens, and between stepping stones. Can also be grown as a house plant. Bonsai gardeners sometimes plant this under Bonsai trees.

Chapter Five

*I have never had so many good ideas day after
day as when I worked in the garden.*
~ John Erskine

Paxton's best friend Jake was sleeping over so
the boys sat at the kitchen table playing some
silly game. Darci had suggested they calm down
and be quiet while she cooked dinner, if they
wanted her to let them stay up to watch the movies they got out of the Redbox kiosk on their way
home. Modern superhero stuff, *The Avengers* or
some version of that, she was pretty sure, *Diary
of a Wimpy Kid,* and some R-rated vampire movie
she'd called Jake's mom to okay. The summary
description said there was mild profanity and vio-
lence but didn't mention lewdness or nudity, so
they agreed the kids could watch it. The boys as-
sured Darci there weren't any of the kissing
vamps and werewolves the silly girls in their class
liked, just the blood sucking kind getting chased

by the good guys.

Darci patted out hamburgers and heated the Fry Daddy for the French fries. With those cooking, she chopped onions and set out the condiments. "Hey, you guys want chocolate milkshakes with supper?"

"Yes please!" Jake had been coming to their house since the boys met in kindergarten and now she thought of him almost like a spare kid. He was as rambunctious as most boys that age, but the thing she liked best about Jake was that he always fessed up when he did something wrong. And he couldn't keep a secret to save his life.

She dipped chocolate ice cream into the blender, then poured milk halfway up the sides. She'd forgot to get the chocolate syrup out of the fridge, so she walked across the room to put up the ice cream and grab it. The boys' silly game caught her attention, and nearly startled the crap out of her. Maybe she ought to take the R-rated movie back. First she had to find out if these sweet little ten-year-olds really were talking about what it sounded like they were talking about.

Booze would follow, either way. Of that she was sure.

"S and M, X X X." Paxton sounded ecstatic. Oh God, if Jake's uncle was responsible for this new interest, she'd go kick his ass herself. Last year his spouting off about 'women's work' was bad enough, but she couldn't imagine him talking to his nephew about anything with a triple X-rating. "What do you think?"

Darci opened the refrigerator and stuck her head inside, pretending to look for something while listening to them over the sound of her heart thumping in her ears. She'd dropped the Hershey's dark chocolate syrup when her son gleefully mentioned S&M.

"Spider-man and Megatron, triple threat! Okay, me next."

Paxton high-fived his best bud. "How'd you know? Okay, your turn."

Darci couldn't remember the last time she'd been so relieved. These boys deserved an extra treat for not being perverted by Jake's uncle, society in general, or the latest top forty music lyrics. She fished out the can of Redi whip and went to the cabinet to get her stash of chocolate sprinkles, both of which she lavished on the shakes as soon as they were poured in the boys' glasses.

"This one's kinda silly. My grandpa says it a lot." Jake finished scratching the pencil against the paper, then slid the page to Paxton.

"L-I-B," Paxton read aloud. "I don't get it. Gimme a sec."

Jake smiled as Paxton scrunched his face up in thought.

"Um, I'll just have to guess." Paxton drew a deep breath, then gave it a shot. "Like it better, lost in Belgium, last is best?"

Jake shook his head, grinning away.

"I give, what's it supposed to mean?"

"Well I'll be!" Jake explained. "Old people say that all the time after somebody does something cool or smart. Um, I lost score, who won?"

"Think it's a draw. We can finish up after supper, if Mom makes us hush up again."

"Time to eat, boys." Darci filled their plates and beamed at Paxton and Jake as they climbed into the bar stools. She walked around behind them, put her arms around them both, and kissed their cheeks despite their protests.

Golden Days Retirement Home had been the first business to hire Petal Pushers for landscaping and upkeep when they opened last year, which ensured them a permanent place in Darci's heart. What she hadn't expected was the lasting friendships she'd made while working there. The elderly had so much to offer, it was a shame some people didn't realize it. She always looked forward to visiting so she could listen to the residents talk about recent events as well as things that took place before her parents were born.

Her two favorite residents were Bernice the gossip queen and Mabel, who refused to let the stroke that put her in the nursing home keep her down.

On this fine spring morning, Darci donned work gloves and cleared off some of the sticks, leaves, and other natural debris that accumulated on the lawn over the winter months. She ached to get her fingers in the fresh herb border, and to bring in new planters for the back yard where some of the residents enjoyed taking their evening meals when weather permitted.

As she pulled up some dead plants and tossed them into the black plastic garbage bag full of leaves and refuse, she realized the past winter must have been harsher than she'd thought, since every one of the rosemary plants had croaked. She'd counted on these perennials to be larger this year, to fill out the border along the sidewalk. No biggie, she'd just have to use larger ones as bedding plants this time round. And with the empty spaces, maybe she could mix in a few new varieties. The chef had often told her she appreciated getting to use these herbs in her menu, and how the residents raved about how much better her soups and fresh pasta dishes tasted once she started adding Darci's fresh herbs to them.

Darci encouraged her to use all she needed. The great thing about herbs is that the more you pinch off, the bushier the plants get.

Mable and Bernice came out to shoot the breeze as Darci finished up. They both wasted no time letting her know things looked tidier and more inviting already, and that she was just as pretty a sight as the tulips blooming under the trees out front.

"I sure am . . . looking forward . . . to spring." Mabel said.

Darci marveled at how far Mabel had come. She still spoke slowly, but the therapy for her speech and mobility had done wonders. Confidence had made the awkward pauses between her words barely noticeable, and there were only a handful of things she couldn't pronounce with ease now. She compensated for the stroke with little tricks she'd learned, and used a tote bag slung over her shoulder to carry things her left hand couldn't grip.

"Be nice to help . . . tend the flowers." Mable's expression suggested embarrassment with her next words. "Sorry all this piled up." She glanced at the open garbage bag. "Afraid I'd pull up something . . . that hadn't greened up, or I'd've started on it."

"Yeah, don't let this heifer fool ya none," Bernice added, with a friendly jibe at her friend. "Mabel's the one who picked up a butt load of twigs from the back yard. A tree fell during that big storm we had a few weeks back. After the maintenance guys sawed it up and hauled it off, this one went behind 'em and cleared away the rest of the mess. "

Darci put a twisty tie around the top of the garbage bag, then took one last scan of the yard. Looked good to her. Now she could take a little break and talk to her friends.

"You know how much I appreciate all your help, Mabel. I've been meaning to ask if you have any ideas or preferences for what y'all would like me to plant this year. Bernice, I remember you saying you were partial to everyday bloomers, so I've put that in my design plan. And plenty of red geraniums, since old Eddy said they were his absolute favorites." Just the mention of these plants made her almost think she could smell fresh dirt and germanium leaves. "And the cook said to grow as much basil as I can stand. Seems she has a recipe for homemade pesto she's itching to whip up in bulk and freeze for use into next winter."

"Well," Mabel said, "my mother had Confederate jasmine . . . by the back gate. Pretty white flowers . . . shaped like tiny stars."

"Oh, I remember that scent, now that you mention it," Bernice said.

"Those would be great!" Darci was already planning where she could put it. Confederate jasmine was pretty easy to grow in partial shade and sun, so that left plenty of spaces around the yard that would be perfect. Just not too close to the roses, though, since those two scents had no business competing with each other. One vining bush could go in the front yard, maybe in a big urn under the tulip poplar tree where Mabel liked to sit and read. Another could go in the back by the patio, since it would be heavenly to catch a whiff of it on summer evenings as residents watched lightning bugs and listened to the crickets chirp. "I do believe I can work a couple of those into the landscape."

The first thing she was going to do when she got back to the shop was call Vera Thompkins to find out which window was Mabel's. She didn't want anyone to hear her asking about it and spoil the surprise. Maybe she could have Bernice lure Mabel into a late night bingo game while Darci and Hoyt planted it right outside her window. She could clear permission to sneak in really late to do it, and make sure Mabel's window was left open, weather permitting, so she could wake up to the scent the next morning.

Bernice got busy repeating all the juicy gossip she'd heard in the past week. Audrey Knickerbocker's granddaughter got knocked up by the mailman. "Isn't that a kicker!" She laughed and slapped her thigh. "It seems it isn't a big deal in this day and age to spit out a kid or two without the luxury of a wedding ring, but still. How ironic is it that prim and too proper to poop Audrey has a twenty-year-old granddaughter who really did get a special delivery from the mailman! Just like in all those bad jokes and pornos!" She flashed an expression like maybe she'd told on herself. "Not that I'd ever watch crap like that, but my late husband had a couple videos he broke out every now and then. Anyway, Mr. Mailman is married, at least until his wife gets a whiff of what he's been up to."

Darci sometimes thought, after her conversations with Bernice, that some of the residents reverted to the naughty versions of their teenage selves, even raunchier now in their golden years than they ever would've dared to be sixty years ago. At least now they couldn't be grounded.

"Janie Geller has been making cow eyes at that old coot, Norman Jones!" Bernice leaned in a little closer, lest someone overhear what she'd most likely already talked to every single resident about. "Beats anything I ever saw, and lord only knows what the heck she sees in him. The orderly let it slip that Norman has hemorrhoids the size of tennis balls, so he has to sit on one of those donut pillows. Then again, Ole Janie has a flatulence problem and spits out the Beano from her medicine cup as soon as the nurse turns her head. Ha! A love made in proctologist heaven, I guess."

"Oh, you're awful," Mabel said, laying her fingertips on her friend's elbow, grinning as she spoke.

"Hey, speaking of scandals, I have something I was wondering if you two could help me with." Darci took off her work gloves and picked up the trash bag. "I'll be right back. Just have to put this in the van and get some papers I want to show you. Can y'all grab us a seat over on the benches by the roses?"

"Sure thing," Bernice said as she and Mabel began to make their way from the front of the building to the seating area off to the side. The bench was flanked by Knockout Roses Darci and Hoyt had set out last year.

Darci trotted back across the yard with a clipboard, hands cleaned off with lemon-scented antibacterial waterless hand soap she kept in the van. Each time the Bath & Body had a sale on the purse-sized containers, she and Charlotte stocked up. No better way to keep the germs away than while sampling the store's latest fragrances.

She gave them a brief summary of Ellen's letter and their meeting, then elucidated on the details as she took out the Betsy list. "If y'all could look over this and point out any surnames you think were common in Webster County at the turn of the century, the early 1900s, that is, it would really help. Charlotte and me already marked the ones we recognized. Oh, here's a green highlighter. Remember, just the ones in the groom column, since we already know Betsy's maiden name. It's her married one we're looking for."

"Y'all are thinking this fella died when?" Bernice asked as she took the clipboard and highlighter. Mabel adjusted her glasses on her nose, all the better to peer through her bifocals.

"In August of 1905, three days after his twin girls were born. Betsy's family is almost positive their great-granddaddy and his family were from Webster County, where the birth happened." Darci smacked herself in the forehead. "Duh! I forgot to tell you Miss Addie Brown was the midwife. She used to live in the house where my flower shop is."

Both ladies turned their gaze toward Darci. Mabel spoke. "Oh, we knew her. Sweet lady. She delivered . . . little ole me in 1935."

"Ha! Me too! Except I'm about a year younger than you, Mabel." Bernice smiled. "We lived just a few blocks from her back then. My aunt was good buddies with her daughter, Virginia I believe her name was. Her oldest boy was quite the looker. Remember him, Mabel?"

They winked at each other as Bernice elbowed Mabel. Darci hoped she was this full of life at their age, and she could just about picture herself and Charlotte bunking together in their blue hair years, playing all kinds of pranks on the staff.

"A-hem." Mabel drew their attention back to the clipboard. "Let's see. Old Webster County names. Rice, Davis . . . the Pooles."

"Yep, Lisman too." Bernice highlighted them. "And Nalls."

As they marked away, Darci asked, "So, do you remember any talk of a man up and disappearing, dying quickly, or spontaneously combusting after his Cherokee wife gave birth?"

"Sorry, but that was thirty years before our time." Mabel's speech flowed more smoothly when her mind was occupied. She pointed to the list.

"Yep, Crowley, I must've skipped right over that one." Bernice highlighted the name. "None of this riddle rings any bells for me either, I'm afraid. I'll think on it and let you know if I can figure anything out about it."

"Thanks. I really appreciate it."

"Heck, I'll ask around, see if one of these old geezers know anything. In this little town, somebody should have overheard their parents or somebody talking about a thing like this." Bernice spoke with the voice of experience. "Um, you will let us know how all this turns out, won't you, honey?"

"Of course I will."

Darci hung up the phone. She wasn't surprised to see Charlotte waiting for an update.

"Ellen had good news. Mrs. James found descendants for an L. S. Jefferson." Darci jotted down the information as she relayed it to Charlotte. She'd forward the email on to Hattie, through Gene's account, later that afternoon. "They even live in northern Pennsylvania. She's supposed to meet with them this Thursday."

"Do they know anything about Betsy?"

"No. But if this pans out, it looks like L. S. had another daughter born the year after Betsy thought her husband died." Darci rolled her eyes. "Looks like philandering went on way back then, too. She promised to call me right after the meeting."

"I hope everything turns out for the best, whether Betsy had her facts straight or not." Charlotte removed some brown leaves from a cluster of African violets in a blue and white pot. "It's sad either way, for Betsy, but Ellen and her family might gain some cousins out of the deal."

Darci swiveled around to face the computer, to finish adding more pictures to Petal Pushers' website. Wreaths made with moss and live herbs were their new best seller online and in the shop. They were beautiful, easy to care for, and smelled divine. If hung where they'd get at least a few hours of sun, and with just a light misting each day, the plants on the wreath should live all season.

She'd also decided to sell herb seedlings online. A lot of people capitalized doing this on eBay and other web outlets, so that was an option. All the holiday wreaths she'd sold through Petal Pushers' website that past winter were a testament to the power of internet sales.

Heirloom vegetables and flower slips were where she'd put her biggest expectations. She'd ordered special seeds and had ten more flats sprouting in the greenhouse. She was especially proud of the assortment of tomatoes. It didn't sound very impressive, but there were some very beautiful, unique varieties in black, purple, and striped orange and yellow, from giant ones down to the tiniest grape variety. The feedback had all been good so far, since the little seedlings made it to their new homes in one piece.

Charlotte was waiting on a customer who wanted a pretty leafy plant for her living room, something colorful, but hard to kill. Her beagle liked to eat plants so it'd have to be non-poisonous, without any prickles or thorns. Spot had tried to munch on her potted cacti last week but was fine now, after the vet spent an hour picking cactus needles out of his mouth.

With a medium sized pot of coleus in her arms, Charlotte walked the lady to the register.

"Oh, how pretty!" The brunette customer pointed to the hanging baskets Darci had put together with some of the year's first annuals. She'd had Wade add a ton of hooks all around the shop to put them on, and the display was quite striking already, with a just a few pots dangling.

After taking a few minutes to decide which she liked best, the lady added a hanging basket to her purchase. Charlotte rang up the sale as the woman rattled off questions. "How do you know how many to put in a pot and which flowers will look good together? What's this weird looking stuff that makes up the bottom?"

"That stuff is made out of coconut husk." Darci stood up to talk to the customer, recognizing a budding passion for plants and flowers in the woman across the counter. She answered the other questions, and made sure to personally hand her a business card. The girl seemed hooked on her new hobby and Darci didn't want to lose her business to Wally World.

"Gee Darce," Charlotte said when the customer left, "if you charged a dollar for every question you answer for customers like her, you'd have those greenhouses paid off in no time."

"Well, that would probably pay better than the pole dancing idea."

Back in front of the computer, she typed a few words before her hands froze over the keyboard. After a few minutes of sitting in a daze, she scribbled her thoughts on a piece of scrap paper, then stood up and started pacing, rolling a pencil between her palms.

"This just might work." Darci hugged Charlotte tight enough to pop her back.

"What? Breaking me in two?" Charlotte looked at her like she'd lost her mind.

"No, your idea. Here," she said, sticking the paper in her cousin's hand. "Take a look at this. You're right that I answer a blue million questions, but I ran with your suggestion and-"

"What suggestion? I have no idea what I'm seeing here. Is this a shopping list?" Charlotte shook her head. "I don't get it, so slow your roll a little."

"Fine." Darci took a deep breath and tried to organize the thoughts buzzing through her mind. "We can teach a class, and that paper in your hand has my ideas for topics to cover. Oh wait, give it back a sec." She snatched it, added something, then handed it back. "*That* alone should make it worth a person's time."

"Oooooh, now I get it." Charlotte studied the notes, and made a couple of her own. "How much are you gonna charge?"

Darci added a figure at the top of the page. "Is that too much?" Her thumb nervously worked the pencil eraser. "What do you think?"

"With the landscape design, hell no." Charlotte took the pencil away from Darci before she could break it. "That, along with the classes, and your students will be getting a bargain."

"I'm thinking the course could run about two months, with classes here every other week." Darci was so excited, she knew she was talking too fast. "We'll supply all the materials, which won't cost us hardly anything, but each student will leave with projects they'll be proud of each time. For the design, they can bring in some pictures of the area they want landscaped, and I'll set up appointments for one-on-one consultations."

"And they'll most likely buy the shrubs and plants from Petal Pushers." Charlotte wiggled her eyebrows. "You're an evil genius. Wait, are you including labor in this fee? Somebody might want to stick a deluxe koi pond in their backyard and that could add up."

"Yeah, good idea. Better specify something like two hours of labor, and hope most of them want to be hands on." Darci added that to her nearly full scrap of paper. "Ten students should just about cover a third of the cost of one greenhouse, a little more if we figure in the landscaping materials they'll need. I may be able to actually pay this off in about the same time I'd hoped to clear the original. Unless another disaster hits."

"When do we start?" Charlotte asked, rubbing her hands together.

"I have absolutely no idea, since I just thought the whole thing up a minute ago." Darci glanced at the calendar on the wall. "As soon as possible. Tonight I'll whip something up to put on the website. Maybe we can mail the class information out to some of our regulars, and we'll post fliers around town."

The phone rang.

"Hi Darci, how's everything going in your world today, honey?"

Darci instantly recognized the voice of one of her favorite people. She wondered what was up, but by the cheerful tone in Bernice's voice, she didn't figure anything too dire was going down.

"If I was any better, I don't think I'd be able to stand myself." Okay, she had to admit that little joke probably sounded better coming from her godfather Max, his favorite response to the how are you question. "How are things at Golden Days?"

"We're all fine, honey. Mabel even better than

most." Bernice's laughter floated through the telephone lines, or maybe it was more accurate to say floated through the signal tower. "She got to spend the whole morning outside, reading under that big poplar tree she likes so much. Surprised her behind didn't go numb, 'cause that bench ain't at all too comfortable. Thought I'd warn you the book is a new one about alternative gardening techniques, so lord only knows what ideas it'll put in her head. She looked pretty content, though."

"Glad to hear it, and I'm sure anything she thinks is interesting enough to share with me, I'll probably take to heart." Darci remembered last year, when she first met her Golden girls, as she sometime thought of Mabel and Bernice. Mabel had been hiding behind a magazine on that very bench, watching Darci work. When Darci tried to talk to her, she'd been so worried about the condition the stroke had left her in, she practically ran past her, with the help of her cane, to get back inside and out of her sight.

"What kind of mischief have you been up to? Don't you dare tell me none, because I know you way better than that." It was so nice to take a break this morning to talk to her friend.

"Well, I declare, I do believe you've got my number, girl." Another of Bernice's bawdy laughs came through the receiver. "Actually, I've been working on that puzzle of yours."

"Puzzle?" Darci thought for a second. "Oh yeah, you're talking about the whole Betsy's baby daddy thing. That's great. What did you come up with?"

"Nothing big, so don't go getting your hopes up." Bernice took a deep breath. "I've been asking around about the stuff you told us about. Asking folks around here if they remembered hearing tell of a man up and disappearing or dropping off the radar right after his wife spit out little twin baby girls. Most folks were like me and Mabel, and just flat out had no idea."

"I feel a big 'but' coming in that pause," Darci said.

"Right you are. I had one old fart who acted mighty strange about it." Bernice chuckled again. "And no, he's not of 'em who's off his nut with old age or the dementia."

Darci was ashamed of herself for a second, because that was the first scenario that had popped into her mind, some crazy old coot sending them on a wild goose chase. "Do I know this old fart, as you so eloquently referred to your friend?"

"I don't rightly know, but he's not any friend of mine. Known him most of my life, lucky me, since he was two grades ahead of me in school. He took to being a bully and never quite got it out of his system. Purt near every night he takes over the TV in the lounge, unless the orderly steps in to remind him about the taking turns rule."

"And his name is? What did he say?" Darci'd been sitting at the counter, but her growing excitement drove her to stand up and pace around the shop. Daisy paused her tweeting to bobble her head when Darci passed.

"He's Charlie Clydell. He never amounted to

much, compared to his kin, but I imagine you recognize the name." Bernice paused, as she liked to do when dropping a gossip bomb, building tension before she lit into the juiciest part.

"Is he related to Stetson Clydell, the one who's running for State Representative when fall rolls around?"

"Yep," Bernice said. "Charlie is Stetson's daddy."

"Wade is doing some work up at his place, adding a closet and such, ripping out a few walls." Darci decided not to even bring up the part about the closet going in that place, or else she never would get off the tangent. "So what weird thing did Charlie say when you questioned him about all this?"

"He clammed his big mouth shut and swole up like a dang toad frog, is what he did." Bernice took another deep breath, which let Darci know there was more to follow. "I was talking to Gail Little about it before I got to him. Noticed him leaning over in his chair, trying to eavesdrop on us, making little huffin' noises the whole time. Got on my nerves so bad I asked him was he having an asthma attack. He just huffed again and leaned the other way."

Gotta love Bernice and her snappy comebacks.

"When I moved on to ask him about it, he was rude as all get out." Bernice huffed herself, showing her disgust for the old coot. "Said he ain't never heard of such a thing, asked why were we messing in a matter that wasn't any of our business, with folks nobody ever heard of in the first

95

place."

"What a lovely man," Darci said sarcastically. "What else did he say?"

"He went on about how this all sounded like a bunch of bull poo and nonsense to him. Guess that's why he had his nose all out of joint about it. He said people should let sleeping dogs lie, BS or not. Then he sorta hung himself."

"You're killing me with suspense." Darci stood gazing out the porthole window, her mind's eye visualizing the whole scene. She didn't have a clue as to what Charlie looked like, but his image was represented by the crabby old man with squinty eyes from the Muppets. "Spill it already, please."

"He said he couldn't figure out why people would care about some fool who gallivanted around with some skanky Indian woman." Bernice said this so proudly, like it was a gem of information.

"But how did he hang himself?" Darci was confused. Maybe Bernice got a hold of the wrong medicine cup this morning. "Ellen told me Cherokees were discriminated against real bad back then, so that's not too shocking, except that it's kind of sad Charlie's so prejudiced at his age."

"But you see, honey," Bernice said, and Darci could visualize the expression on her friend's face perfectly, even through the phone. Bombshell on the way. "I never mentioned that Betsy was a Cherokee. Me nor Mabel either one."

Goose bumps rose on Darci's arms. "Oh my goodness."

"Yep, not only is he lying about not knowing anything, he's got too many details about something that happened a hundred and some years ago."

"Have I told you lately that I love you, Bernice?"

"Not nearly enough, but the feeling's mutual. So, what should we do next?" Bernice paused for a second. When she spoke again, it was mock gangsta style. "You want me and Mabel should highjack his meds, put some hurt on him til he talks?"

Darci laughed. The odd thing was, she wasn't all together convinced Bernice was joking.

Petal Pushers Plant Profile for Confederate Jasmine

Trachelospermum jasminoides
Perennial vine

Confederate jasmine is also called star jasmine.

Brief description: This evergreen is famous for its intoxicating scent. The blooms look like clusters of little white stars or pinwheels when it blooms from early spring into summer. The leaves are shiny and dark green. It's pest free and drought resistant, and easy to care for.

Trivia: Despite its name Confederate jasmine isn't native to the South, but was brought here from China. Just one of these vines will perfume an entire yard. Oh, they smell so good! Just ask Mabel Guthrie, because it's her favorite.

Growing instructions: This quick growing vine grows best in full sun to partial shade. Pinch it back to give the plant a bushier, fuller appearance.

Uses: Confederate jasmine is a beautiful addition to any landscape. It can be pruned into a hedge, or does very well vining up a light pole or trellis.

Chapter Six

*It is a golden maxim to cultivate the garden for the
nose, and the eyes will take care of themselves.*
~ Robert Louis Stevenson

"Hi Ellen. I've been waiting for your call, thinking
about y'all all afternoon." Darci fidgeted with the
phone cord, eager to hear the news. "So how'd it
go?"

"Fred and his family were super nice. You by
the computer?"

"Yep."

"I just sent you a shot of me with him and his
family." Ellen laughed into the receiver. "Tell me
what you think. A picture's worth a thousand
words, but this one might leave you speechless."

"Okay, email's open and your pic's loading.
Oh." Ellen was right, and Darci found herself not
exactly sure what to say. "Um . . . they have really nice smiles. So. Did your great-granddaddy's
illegitimate daughter marry a Chinese man

named Jefferson, or did Mrs. James send you barking up the wrong family tree?"

"Wrong family, totally, but at least I made some new friends. They got stuck labeled Jefferson when their ancestor came to America and whoever did their paperwork gave up trying to spell a lovely Asian name I'm not even going to try to pronounce." Ellen didn't sound too disappointed. "So, we're back where we started."

No sooner had Darci hung up the land line than her cell buzzed. She picked it up off the counter and touched the cute little Android text message icon, the square green smiling face with a number one on its forehead. The sender was Wade, which she found odd, since he wasn't much for typing things in and usually preferred to just make an old fashioned phone call.

One look at the message made it clear that Paxton was playing with his dad's phone. It started with 'Hey Mom' and contained as many abbreviations as possible. She was going to either have to buy a magic decoder ring or possibly call Jake to help her decipher it. She attempted to read it one more time.

'Hey Mom,

We ct a slw o ><=o>J. Dad sd 2 tl U 2 XX 2ntz brgrs. We'r friN ><=o>J! :P

<3 Pax'

She walked to the kitchen and plopped into a chair beside Charlotte, who sat sipping raspberry tea.

Darci slid the phone with the text message on the screen in front of her cousin. "You have any

102

idea what the heck that's supposed to mean? I get the 'hey mom' and 'love Paxton' parts, but everything in between is making me go cross eyed. Yeah, I know the colon and capital p mean a smiling face with its tongue sticking out."

"When did you give Paxton a cell phone? I thought you were going to put that off as long as possible." Charlotte picked up the smart phone and took a look. "Where's he at, anyway?"

"Not his cell, he's playing on his daddy's. Him and Wade are out fishing again, surprise, surprise. Can you make anything out of that?" Darci asked.

"Well," Charlotte rubbed her forehead. "If Jimbo sent me a text like this I'd swear he was drunk. I doubt Pax is hitting anything harder than Pepsi, so we can rule that out. Hey! You think these are supposed to be fish?" She held the cell so she and Darci could both see it, then pointed to the two parts that looked like '><=o>J'. "You know, like how people draw a bunny hiding in the grass with symbols, on Facebook and Twitter. Wade must be boring that poor kid to death if he had time to figure this out. See here, the last greater than sign could be the head, the other one the tail. Either the equal sign or the 'o' is probably supposed to be a fin or scales or something. "

"How does the capital 'J' fit in?" Darci was seriously about to get a headache.

"That's the easy part. It's a hook, get it?" Charlotte looked rather proud of herself.

"How stupid of me not to get that." Darci's

voice dripped sarcasm. "But I think you're right. Okay, let's figure out that first sentence. 'We ct a slw o ><=o>J'. We something a something o fish. Of fish. We cut a slaw of fish?"

"Caught a slew! Ha!" Charlotte shouted out like she'd just won the lottery. "We caught a slew of fish! That makes a lot more sense that cutting slaw. Paxton royally hated coleslaw, when I put some on his plate last week."

They high-fived.

"Who would've thought you could think like a child." Darci smirked. "On to the next part. What does 'Dad sd 2 tl U 2 XX 2ntz brgrs' mean? Dad is the only thing I can make out. Let's see you work your magic on that."

"Hmmm, those double Xs kinda make you wonder, huh?" Charlotte grinned and wiggled her eyebrows up and down.

"Actually, no. Paxton and Jake were playing some silly game at the house the other night," she explained. "I about pissed myself when I heard Pax say S and M XXX. Then Jake correctly guessed Spiderman and some other superhero who started with an 'M', triple threat or win or something That along with all these weird new abbreviations people keep coming up with for texts is about to make my head explode. But back to this. Only two exes, and I have no idea."

"The three twos obviously just stand for 'to'," Charlotte reasoned. "I tell ya, Darce, if the boy does this to you again, you should punish him with a stationary kit. Make him write things out for a week."

"That's actually not a bad idea." Darci considered it, thinking it would be nice for her son to have experience writing real letters, in case pen and paper should come back in style over texts and emails one day. "The 'U' is for you, I guess."

"So we have 'Dad something to something you to Xs', that doesn't mean anything perverted, '2ntsz something'. Two nuts, two knots," Charlotte pointed to '2nts' as she continued to guess. "Seconds? Ugh."

"Oh no."

"What?" Charlotte asked.

"This part could be Dad sad to tell you. That's all I need, something bad Wade needs to tell me." Darci rubbed her cheek, bracing herself. "Okay, if they'd fell out of the stupid boat or something, I doubt he'd have Paxton text me about it. Unless Wade was unconscious and Pax grabbed the cell."

"I really will have to slap you if you don't calm down and focus." Charlotte shot her a look which suggested she was prepared to do just that. "I have to figure this out now or it'll drive me nuts. 'Sd' probably means said instead of sad. Paxton wouldn't say Dad sad to tell you, for one thing. Doesn't sound like how he talks, plus he'd have put a 'z' after Dad, for Dad's, because Dadz would look way cooler than using an apostrophe 's'. And if they just caught a slew of fish, you know Wade's got that stupid grin plastered across his face."

"You're right, but don't even think about smacking me." Darci shook her finger at her as

105

she spoke. "Now for the 'XX 2 nutz brgrs'. Oh! Burgers! We were going to grill out tonight. Tonight! Ha! Two nutz is tonight! Tonight's burgers."

"Wade wants him to tell you to do something double X rated with tonight's burgers?" Charlotte laughed. "And you say I'm the sicko."

"Ha ha, very funny." But Darci laughed too. "Okay, we caught a slew of fish, Dad said to tell to something tonight's burgers. What do you make of that last sentence? 'We'r friN ><=o>J'?"

Charlotte stared at the text for a few seconds. "We're frying fish! And Jimbo makes fun of me for watching game shows with puzzles like this!"

"But what about the exes and the burgers? Why would they want to have burgers and fish?" Darci asked.

"The exes must me to cross out or forget the burgers," Charotte explained. "See, now this message from hell makes sense. It says 'Hi Mom, We caught a slew of fish. Dad said to tell you to forget tonight's burgers. We're frying fish! Happy face. Love Pax'."

"My god, you've cracked it," Darci said.

"How would you ever make it without me?" Charlotte flashed her wicked grin.

Mrs. Jenkins lived down the street with her calico cat, both of whom could be seen sitting on her porch swing most afternoons, people watching. Darci stood listening to her now, wishing

Bernice would come in so these two could talk each other's ears off. Oh, the funny things she'd overhear from getting those two together.

It was weird, come to think of it, that Bernice and Mrs. Jenkins looked to be about the same age, but one lived in an assisted living environment while the other frailer one lived on her own. The ever gregarious Bernice was as spry now as most thirty-year-olds, and would no doubt tackle a bear with a switch if it was stupid enough to tick her off. Mrs. Jenkins, on the other hand, walked with a cane, the wooden handle well worn from years of helping her keep her balance; she was frail, yet her mind was sharp as a tack, but it was easy to see she was a bit lonely and would benefit from having others around her on a daily basis, up close and conversational, not just those who said hello as they walked past her house.

Mrs. Jenkins had been a regular customer ever since Petal Pushers' big grand opening. The lady truly liked flowers, enjoyed coming in to browse the displays and partake of the cup of coffee, tea, lemonade, or hot cocoa, depending on the weather, that Darci always offered her. Charlotte had come up with the idea about the chair they kept just for her, but of course other customers used it to take a load off when they needed to, as well. Darci and Charlotte went to the big flea market in Greenville early one Tuesday morning, in plenty of time to go and get back before the shop opened at eight am, and found a pair of old chairs that must have once gone with a dining set. The dark wooden parts just needed a little furniture polish rubbed into the grain to bring them back to life, and they picked up two new cushions at Walmart to make them more comfortable. Mrs. Jenkins had a slight figure so Darci figured that with so little padding on her butt, she'd appreciate the cushioning. After they'd shined the wooden chairs up and tied on the padding, they placed one on either side of the doorway leading from the main room of the shop into the kitchen, directly across from the counter on the far side of the room.

Darci often cringed when she sold this nice old lady certain plants, the ones that required maintenance more than once a week. Her first instincts after she'd caught on last year was to steer her toward a rather large selection of cacti in pretty clay pots. Darci offered Mrs. Jenkins a BOGO on it, buy one get one free, but she'd reached out one dainty little old finger, touched the sharp end of a cactus quill, and shook her head. "Oh, no thank you, sweetie," she'd said, with a sweet grin on her face. "My cat would put her eye out on that thing. I'll just stick with that pretty orchid I set by the register."

She'd brought it back in two weeks later, a dead withered stalk with a few crunchy brown leaves clinging to it. The once beautiful pink and white petals had fallen off and now lay on the potting soil like grave markers. Darci'd told her she'd be happy to replace it, perhaps with a jade plant, very elegant and it seldom needed water-ing. Instead, she insisted on a miniature rose bush, to keep inside, to brighten up a dark corner. When Darci explained that these small roses needed full sun to thrive, like in a westward facing window, Mrs. Jenkins shook her head and patted Darci's hand, which had clinched into a fist, nails digging into her palm at the thought of how bad the tiny yellow rose bush would look in ten days. "It'll be fine," Mrs. Jenkins had said. "I saw one just like it on the late night movie channel a few nights ago. They had it growing in a dusty ole study darker than the corner I want to put it in. The area by my windows is already cheery enough, but that corner could use a little brightening up." Darci managed a grin she didn't feel, not wanting to be rude to this lady she actually was quite fond of. She rang up the sale, thinking this was as bad as watching someone else's two-year-old pick up a dainty piece of crystal glassware in the mall; nothing you could do but stand back, grit your teeth, and wait for the crash when it hit the floor.

Today, thank goodness, Mrs. Jenkins was in Petal Pushers to pick up a gift for her great-niece's bridal shower. The shop stocked finer pieces of silver and crystal for just such occasions, and Darci was relieved to show her something that wasn't a living plant for a change. Mrs. Jenkins picked out two beautiful sterling silver candlesticks and a cut glass candy dish. Now standing at the counter, Mrs. Jenkins told Darci about her plans to go to the shower. Her sister was going to pick her up and drive them to the fancy country club in Henderson. They'd be serving smoked salmon and quiches, and her great-niece was marrying a medical student who moved here from Florida.

Darci was happy to see Mrs. Jenkins' excitement, how her eyes seemed to sparkle like tiny diamonds in her blue irises. When she noticed her leaning harder on her cane, she told her to have a seat while she wrapped the shower gifts. Mrs. Jenkins sank into the cushion on the chair by the doorway while Darci went to the back for paper and tape, and brought her a glass of sweet tea to drink while she waited.

When the tea was drained, the gifts wrapped and crowned with curly ribbons, and Mrs. Jenkins was all talked out, Darci rang up the purchases without charging for the wrapping. She tucked two cards under the bows, and pointed them out to Mrs. Jenkins so she wouldn't forget to fill them out before the shower. The big paper bag with handles, which Darci'd got a great deal on a few months before, felt much heavier than she'd expected when filled with the gifts. She didn't think the lady would be able to carry it down the street, even though her house was just a short walk from the shop. It was Hoyt's day off or she'd have had him drop it off for her.

"Charlotte, can you watch the front for a few?" Darci yelled toward the workroom where her cousin was busy filling orders for a hospital patient recovering from back surgery.

"Sure." Charlotte came up front, wiping her hands on her work apron.

"Thanks, I won't be too long." Darci walked toward the front with the older lady, selecting her words with care so as not to make it sound as if she were putting herself out. "Didn't have time to go for my walk this morning-" or the last two weeks either, she thought but wouldn't admit out loud, "-so I thought I'd get one in now." She turned to Mrs. Jenkins.

"You don't mind if I tag along with you, do you?" Darci shifted the bag to the other hand, the one farthest from the elderly lady, so she wouldn't attempt to try and carry it herself.

"Well of course I don't." Mrs. Jenkins smiled as they walked through the door and down the sidewalk. "Glad to have the company."

Darci walked a whole mile afterward, taking the long way back around a few blocks. Mrs. Jenkins wouldn't let her leave after she'd came in, not without letting her pet her cat, or without a piece of lemon cake wrapped in a napkin. Darci ate it on the way back to the shop, which prompted her to walk off a few calories as she licked the cream cheese icing off the napkin.

Back at Petal Pushers she checked her email, then she spent a while on Pinterest, her newest fun way to waste time via the computer. There was never any telling what she'd see on there. She had boards for recipes, Krispy Kreme stuff, new hairstyles she considered letting Donovan try out on her, exercise videos that looked like fun but she doubted she'd ever buy, and gift ideas. Her favorite category was the one for gardening, no surprise, full of pins that covered everything from fairy houses to new hybrids, moss sculptures, and even cool ways to package seeds.

She wanted to figure out how to pin pictures of arrangements and wreaths made at Petal Pushers on Pinterest, to help drum up more business to help pay off her debts. She enjoyed keeping the Petal Pushers website updated with plant profiles and current sales.

Darci scrolled past a picture someone had posted of a group of cell phone covers, one dark mossy green with variegated flower petals downs the side. She looked at it for a minute, trying to decide if she wanted to splurge on one like it. After glancing at her payment booklet, she decided against it. She didn't need to buy anything frivolous until after those greenhouses were paid off. By then phones might be obsolete.

That night Darci, Wade, and Paxton chowed down on some of the best fried catfish they'd ever eaten. Darci was glad Wade knew how to clean the ugly things to get rid of all the bones. Nothing sucked more than a stray bone stabbing you in the jaw.

After the dishes were cleared away, Wade and Paxton settled down on the couch to watch a baseball game. Pulling her fingernails out with pliers would have been more fun to Darci. Unless her son or husband was out there chasing a ball around the field, she couldn't give two hoots in hell about any part of it.

She went upstairs to watch a Lifetime movie in her room. It might be nice to have a cat to keep her company on nights like this, when the men in her life were kidnapped by ESPN. After considering how fun it would be to cuddle up with a kitten, she remembered why it was out of the question. She brought Daisy home with her on long weekends, and no way could she risk something happening to the little parakeet she loved so much. No cat for the Sheltons, end of that.

When the movie took its first commercial break, Darci decided to get herself a snack and look over her Betsy notebook. No one had came up with anything new in over a week, but she truly hoped the others weren't getting discouraged. Sometimes it just took a while to figure things out.

She snuggled in the bed, sitting up with pillows fluffed between her back and the headboard. A saucer with two Krispy Kreme donuts waited beside her on the bed and a tall glass of chocolate milk sat on a coaster on the nightstand. She moved the remote so it wouldn't get wet if she spilled the milk, then put Wade's pillow on her lap to prop up the notebook as she leafed through it. "Huh, how did that get in there," she said when an elongated leaf off some kind of shrub fell from between the pages.

"Hey, Mom," Paxton said from the doorway to her room.

"What's up, Pumpkin Butt?"

"Mo-om." Paxton stretched her name out until it was almost a whine. "For cryin' out loud. I hate it when you call me that."

"Can't help it, I have to pick on my favorite people." Darci blew him a kiss, which he sidestepped. "How else would you know I love you?"

The boy let out a huff, then shook his head as

113

if it wouldn't be worth his time to disagree.

"Oh heck." It dawned on her that she was doing to her son the very same thing Hoyt did to her. She was just as bad. "Pax, wouldn't it hurt your feelings if I stopped calling you my little pet names?"

"It's embarrassing when you call me stuff in front of my friends," he paused for a deep breath, "but I don't want to make you mad enough to stop, I don't guess."

Darci couldn't believe it took a chat with Paxton for her to understand why Hoyt would not quit with the Boss Lady bit. She thought of him as a little brother, and he most likely thought of her as a big sister. Or, she gulped and sighed, as a mother figure. Either way, she guessed she'd lay off asking him to quit, but not enough so it took the fun out of it for him.

"By the way," Darci said, changing the subject as she remembered something she'd meant to talk to him about. "It took me a while to figure out what your text message meant today, with a lot of help from Charlotte. Next time, just remember I don't keep up with latest text slang, and maybe keep it a little more simple, if you don't mind."

"Sure. I forget you didn't have anything but those big funny looking phones when you were a kid." The sad thing about Paxton's little speech is he was being serious. "Back in the olden days."

Darci felt like she was a hundred and twelve. "We did have TV."

"Yeah, the big black and white ones, with wires

on top but no remotes or DVRs, like on the old Andy Griffith show, right?"

Kill me now, she thought. "Yeah, they invented those right after the wheel."

"Oh yeah," Paxton said, remembering something. "The reason I came up here is me and Dad were gonna get a snack but there was only one donut left. He told me to ask if you were saving it or if I could have it." Paxton rolled his eyes. "Didn't think you cared, but Dad said it was rude to gobble up the last of anything without asking other people if they wanted it."

"That's sweet, but you can have the last donut." She held up her plate to show him hers with one big bite taken out of it. "See, I beat you to the snacks."

"Thanks."

"Enjoy your game," Darci said as he turned to go back downstairs. "Hope your team wins."

She heard Wade and Paxton cheer a few minutes later, and assumed the boys' team, whichever one that was she didn't know, got a home run or a good hit or something. Sports were not her thing.

Darci shifted her attention between the movie and the Betsy dilemma.

She took the list of grooms out of the binder—she'd had to upgrade from the folder when papers started falling out—and read over it for the umpteenth time. A dozen or more surnames were highlighted to indicate names common to Webster County at the turn of the nineteenth century. Nothing new there so she moved on to the other documents. It was a good thing Shane had suggested using the women's names instead of all that grandma and great-grandma jazz. Still, a lot of the information was repetitive and it was tiresome to reread 'Betsy's husband, real name unknown'.

She ought to let Paxton come up with abbreviations for some of that stuff, but then figured he might make it more confusing.

A thought hit her about the text from hell she and Charlotte deciphered, and the game Paxton and Jake had played. She snatched up the list and read over the names more slowly this time, then flipped through the notes Ellen gave her after meeting with the genealogist and historian, the movie totally forgotten by this point. With a pen from her nightstand and some lined paper from the back of the binder, she jotted down the main names in this puzzle, with single quotes to show the aliases: Betsy Hicks 'McGee'; 'L. S. McGee'; the twins, Ella and Emma, neither with middle names.

Had Betsy left a clue in the initials she gave her late husband? Charlotte was better with puzzles but if she called her now it might wake little Cole up, and then her poor cousin never would get any sleep.

"Hmmmm." Darci's thumb played across the top of the pen, clicking the ball point in and out as she talked to herself. "Ella and Emma. Ella and Emma. Can't believe I didn't notice that before." The twins' names sounded like the letters 'L' and 'M'.

She scribbled some more on her note paper, playing around with the letters. She didn't even know for sure if 'L'a and 'M'a was a significant find. L. S. still pretty much had her stumped. "What name could a person possibly get out of that? Els? I think not." Darci huffed, then picked the Betsy list back up. Quite a few of the grooms listed had initials, some instead of the first name, some instead of the second. Logan Simms and Lenard Stillwater had been crossed out after the genealogist checked them out, since both lived to be old men who died way after the 1920s, years after Betsy's man went belly up.

She starting at the top of the list and said each name out loud, looking for any possible connection to the letter sounds in the girls' names as well as their father's.

After about fifteen minutes of that, Darci felt sorry for people who did that kind of thing for a living. How much would researchers get paid to pour over old records of people related to some client they barely knew. She hoped they were well compensated, because the thought of having a job like that would make her pull her hair out.

She rubbed her eyes and finished off her donut. The movie was still on, though she hadn't been paying any attention to it this past half hour.

Next she wrote out each of the highlighted names common to Webster County, doodling with them as she stared at the little family tree she'd drawn at the top of the page, with Betsy, L. S., Ella and Emma, drawing little roots and leaves as she concentrated. A cute little family tree took shape as Darci sketched roots and leaves around the first words she'd written.

Just when she was about to cram the papers back into the binder and slam it shut, she froze, her gaze drawn to a name she'd missed. The one written above it was also highlighted in green, and her eyes had mistakenly thought the line was just heavy; now it became clear that this other name was marked though a bit above center.

"Oh . . . My. . . God." Darci wrote the name at the top of the page, with arrow doodles connecting it to L. S., Ella, and Emma.

"Ha! This is it!" She jumped out of bed and did a little victory dance around the room.

"You alright up there, Hon?" Wade must have heard the commotion, but was too caught up in his ball game to walk upstairs to check on her.

"I'm fine," Darci hollered back down. "Just excited, because I just figured out who Betsy's husband was."

She picked up the phone, then reached for Ellen's number in her notes. "Damn it!" She hung up, since it was past ten o'clock and she was pretty sure Pennsylvania was an hour ahead of that. Receiver in hand, she considered dialing anyway, since Ellen would want to know as soon as possible, but manners won out.

Now she'd have to wait until morning to share the news. She traced over her discovery with the ink pen until the words almost jumped off the page.

"Ellis Milton Clydell," she said out loud.

Both of the twins' names started with an 'E', but Ella sounded so much like Ellis, it couldn't be a coincidence. Emma might have been meant to be a clue to her daddy's middle name.

Ellis sounded like L. S. This could be all wrong, but she had a gut feeling about it. Best thing to do was have Ellen call Mrs. James in the morning and ask her to check the records for Ellis Clydell, to see where he was from or who his parents were.

If she was right and Ellis Milton Clydell was their Betsy's husband, they'd finally have a name for the missing link in Ellen's family.

Even if this turned out to be the right man, they still had to find out what happened to him, as well as why his family was out to get Betsy and the girls.

If the twins really were long lost Clydells, how would Stetson and Charlie react to the news?

Three Sisters Garden
Class handout

Not only is this a space-saving way to grow beans, corn, and pumpkins, it looks really cool.

What you'll need:
Corn seeds
Pole bean seeds
Pumpkin or winter squash seeds

1) Till the soil as you would for a regular garden. You'll need a round area at least eight feet in diameter. Plant corn seed about inch deep, spacing them about five inches apart in a large circle in the center of your prepared spot. Water them, and wait for them to sprout and grow a couple of inches.

2) Plant your pole bean seeds in a ring about six inches outside of your corn, sowing them an inch deep and spacing about five or six inches apart. Water and wait for them to grow.

3) Then come back and plant your winter squash or pumpkins about a foot away from your beans, about an inch deep. Water them, and they'll be up in no time.

4) As the beans grow, wrap them around the corn stalks. You can position the ends of the squash or pumpkin vines so they stay pretty much inside the circle.

5) Enjoy

Chapter Seven

You can't be suspicious of a tree,
or accuse a bird or a squirrel of a subversion
or challenge the ideology of a violet.
~ Hal Borland

"Mornin' Charlotte," Darci said as soon as her cousin set foot in the main room. Daisy perched on her shoulder, where she'd sat listening to Darci blab nonstop for the past half hour.

"Good morning to you too, Little Darci Sunshine." Charlotte walked past her, greeted Daisy with a kissy sound, then took a seat in one of the office swivel chairs. "You look well caffeinated."

"No, I'm still on my first cup."

"Well, that goofy grin on you face would suggest you've been up to something. Spill it before you bust."

"I thought you'd never ask. I would've kicked your butt if you'd picked today to come in late or call in sick." Darci could feel herself practically bubbling over with enthusiasm.

"You know that hardly ever happens. I should get an award for missing the least amount of work while raising my first kid."

"I know, I appreciate it, and I apologize for switching the subject right back to my big news." Darci pointed to the counter, her Betsy binder opened and oozing information. "Take a look, and you'll see what I figured out last night. And you're welcome, since I didn't call you right then and wake up Cole."

"Oh my God! You found Betsy's long lost hubby!" Charlotte picked up the page and seemed impressed. "You sure it's him?"

"My gut tells me I'm right, and Miss Addie's hinting at it. You know I talk to the bird, and myself, all the time. Before you got here I told Daisy my theory about Ellis Milton Clydell." Darci grinned as she ran her hand over the fresh goose bumps on her bare arms. "Just like now, I got a cold spot and a tweeting frenzy. Let me put her in the cage and I'll explain all the arrows."

Still chirping away, the parakeet hopped from her swing to the side of the cage as if expecting some unseen person to open her little door and take her back out. Darci pointed a thumb in Daisy's direction. "Miss Addie is in the house."

"I see what you mean." Charlotte reached under the counter for a blanket she stowed there to help cope with the cold spots. They'd stopped being creeped out by the ghost long ago, since she managed to help them out, sometimes more than they immediately realized. "Now explain your scribbles."

Well, it's about time! I swany, sometimes I think these folks must be either stone deaf or not too bright. There I stood beside Darci the other day, a-yellin' the man's name in her ear, but she heard nary a word I had to say. Made me feel like a dog a-waggin' its tail at a blind man.

My life sure would be a whole lot easier if she learned how to pay attention to what all I'm tryin' to tell her. For now, though, I'm just happy she's got the right name. Ella and Emma, those sweet little girls deserve to know the truth about their daddy.

Darci went over how she'd figured everything out the night before. "And look here, the girls' names sound like the letters 'L' and 'M'. Ella and Emma, get it?"

"Sort of." Charlotte nodded.

"Betsy named them after their dad, since Ella and Ellis are spelled so similar, and the 'M' sound in Emma could stand for Milton."

Charlotte stayed quieter than usual, which made Darci worry that she might be wrong.

"You think?"

"The Ellis part I think you've got right. The girls' names and his middle one and stuff, I'm not sure if that was planned or a coincidence or what," Charlotte said. "What did Ellen say?"

"Haven't called her yet." Darci gathered all the

papers up in front of her. "Pass me that phone and I'll get right on it."

Ellen was psyched during their phone conversation, to put it mildly. Darci could hear pages rustle in the background and imagined she was sketching her own little picture and arrows as Darci explained her line of thought.

"Thank you, thank you, thank you! I'm gonna call Mrs. James right now and ask if she can check this Ellis M. Clydell's records to see if we can prove he's my great-granddaddy. This is so exciting!" Ellen muffled the phone and woo-hooed to prove it.

She promised to let Darci know the instant she heard anything.

Darci's next call was to Hattie. No surprise when the temperature dropped again as soon as Miss Addie's granddaughter's voice sounded through speaker phone. Hattie was nearly as thrilled as Ellen had been.

"You know, Grandma couldn't stand any of those Clydells, but I never knew what they'd done to get her so riled up." Hattie clucked her tongue. "If they're the ones responsible for trying to hurt her friend Betsy and those babies, I can sure see why she hated them. Oh me, I wish I could go back in time to ask her about all this. I guess there are some things we'll just never know."

So Miss Addie, who everyone said had a loving disposition and was loved by all, had loathed the Clydells. Maybe they were on the right track, but how would they ever figure out the details? Damn, Darci wished somebody would write a book called *Teaching Your Ghost to Talk for Dummies.*

Darci almost asked if she'd had a chance to go through Miss Addie's old storage boxes. She decided against it, afraid it would make Hattie feel bad if she hadn't, or push her to overexert herself. She asked how Hattie's husband Gene was feeling instead. She'd mentioned his back problems the last time she'd come down.

"Oh, he's doing a little better. The doctor gives him a cortisone shot every so often. Got him to help me paint the porch swing last week, so he's making it pretty well," Hattie said.

"Glad to hear that he's on the mend."

"Oh, I meant to tell you, I got my grandson to haul a few of those old boxes and trunks in for me the other day when they were visitin'. You wouldn't believe the memories that came up after all these years, just handling small things that my grandparents once touched." Hattie's voice held a special touch of nostalgia. "Mostly just old everyday cookware, you know, those big aluminum pots and strainers and such. Found some cookie cutters she used to let me help her cut cookie dough with, and her rolling pins. Had Gene help me arrange them in a shadowbox in the dining room. Looks real nice. And one of her recipe books was on the bottom of the box, wrapped up in an old tea towel. Miracle the mice didn't get to it."

"Was it one of those red and white checkered *Better Homes and Gardens* editions? They've been around for years, I think." Darci had a pretty nice cookbook collection of her own. A person couldn't have too many dessert recipes.

"It's a bound book that came with blank pages. Grandma copied her favorites in there by hand mostly, like her corncob jelly recipe on the second page, and glued in clipping from magazines and such." There was that wistful tone again, and it made Darci smile. "I've only looked through a few pages. I'm saving the full read through for Saturday morning. At my age, it's fun to plan things out."

"Don't suppose there were any letters between her and Betsy tucked in with the cookware."

"Afraid not. But I promised myself I'd go through a few of those boxes each week, and I'm actually looking forward to it. No tellin' what I'll find."

Daisy lit into a twittering fit.

Darci glanced at the mosaic clock and smiled.

The next afternoon, Darci got an email from Ellen with a file attached. She hollered for Charlotte to hurry up and haul herself out of the bathroom so they could read the news, whatever it may be, together.

"Gees, Darce, give a girl a minute, will ya?" Charlotte walked into the main room, still fastening her belt. "Glad I'm not constipated or you'd really get your panties in a wad."

The email itself was short and sweet. Ellen had been able to get Mrs. James, for an extra fee, to drop what she'd been doing to look up anything she could find about the Ellis Milton Clydell who married Betsy Hicks in 1904.

Mrs. James hit pay dirt.

The attachment was a copy of the original marriage bond between Ellis and Betsy. The old fashioned handwriting could be a bit hard to read, so the genealogist had included a transcription. Now they had proof Ellis Milton Clydell married Ellen's great-grandmother, plus they had the names and birthplaces of both his parents.

Darci pulled into the driveway at Golden Days Retirement Home the next day. She opened the van door, then went around to the back of it to unload some new planters, a couple flats of Wave petunias, and other flowers she planned to fill them with. The dolly wheels sank into the grass as she made a few trips to the patio, especially when hauling the ginormous pots that made her wish it'd been one of Hoyt's mornings to work instead of his class day. She was just lucky he'd decided to stay on working at Petal Pushers after he graduated high school last year. He clocked between twenty-five and forty hours a week, depending on his academic work load, more during the summer and any breaks in the college calendar.

Bernice and Mabel joined her after she filled the rustic concrete planters with potting soil—never mind that she'd almost busted a gut wiggling the things off the dolly—and the ladies sat and chatted with her as she arranged and rearranged the petunias, snapdragons, stevia, and ivy until she got it the way she wanted. Trowel in hand, she made little holes and promptly set the flower slips in the first planter. She could tell Mabel was itching to get her hands in the project, but was too shy to ask if she could help.

Rubbing her lower back, Darci stood up and stretched, then added a little fake groan for good measure. "Think I might have strained something in my dang back, when I yanked that big sack of dirt out of the van." She twisted sideways, hoping her acting skills were convincing.

"Don't wear . . . yourself out, Darci," Mabel said, leaning forward on her cane. "Need help?"

She knew one of her elderly friends hadn't been fooled for a split second, since Bernice sat angled slightly behind the other woman, a broad grin on her face as she winked at Darci.

"I'd love some help, if it wouldn't be putting you out any." Darci pulled a fresh pair of gardening gloves out of her work apron, which was actually one of Wade's old cloth tool belts. Mabel took them and the gardening trowel, then carefully sat on the overturned bucket Darci'd used for a chair. "Thanks so much."

Mabel's face lit up as she picked up a red and white striped petunia, sank the little shovel into the soil, and set the flower in the new hole, her aged fingers gently tamping the soil in place around the plant. She was in her element.

"I actually moved my trip here up little, since I got a certain phone call yesterday." Darci grinned as both her friends turned their eyes toward her.

"Well, let us in on it, honey." Bernice was on

the edge of her seat, eager to gobble up any gossip Darci had to offer. "We ain't gettin' any younger, don't you know."

"I wondered if you had . . . any news about that," Mabel said, still happily working in the new rustic concrete planter.

"Take it y'all guessed the news is from Ellen."

"Well, duh, honey." Bernice sat up straighter. "We haven't gone senile yet."

"Okay, I won't keep y'all in suspense any longer." Darci filled them in on how she'd figured out Betsy's husband's name.

"I can't believe it took the lot of us that long before somebody figured it out. L. S. does sound just like Ellis," Bernice said. "Did you work out what the rest of his name was?"

"Oh yes I did." Darci explained how she'd gone over the list the other night paying special attention to all the names they'd highlighted as being possible Webster County residents. "So the man known by his descendant as L. S. McGee for the past hundred and some years was actually named . . ." Darci let the tension build because it was so much fun to finally be the one with exciting news for a change. Now she could understand what a thrill Bernice got from swapping stories.

"Darci, don't you make me call your Grandmama Odette and let her know you're up here at the old folk's home tormenting us." Bernice slapped her thigh and cackled. Darci realized that even now, at thirty-some years old, she still must have got a pretty worried expression on her face at the threat of upsetting her grandmother.

"Just kiddin', honey, unless you don't hurry on up and tell us."

"His name was . . . Ellis Milton Clydell!" Darci watched as Mabel and Bernice exchanged surprised glances.

"I knew that old fart Charlie was acting peculiar as all get out!" Bernice leaned against the back of her bench, stretching her arms out along the wooden slats. "Mabel, what relation do you reckon he is to Betsy's Ellis?"

"I have no idea." The right corner of Mabel's mouth turned up in a grin as she planted a snapdragon. "That was before my time."

"Well, yeah, mine too, but I figured since the Clydells are distant cousins of yours, you might know a little something something."

Darci giggled at Bernice's choice of words, considering what 'something something' usually meant. Then she felt her eyes widen at the realization that that might be exactly what Bernice meant. Nobody could say she wasn't still full of piss and vinegar, even at her age.

"Afraid not." Mabel shook her head.

"Ain't no tellin' what they'll dig up on those Clydells," Bernice said, eyes blaring. "No offense to your family twig off that branch, Mabel."

"None taken," Mabel shot back. "Those boys were . . . mean as snakes."

"Well, we do have Ellis' dad's name," Darci said, thinking it was cool Mabel had a family connection to the whole mess, though she wasn't surprised. Roots in Webster County ran deep and spread wide. "Does the name Titus Clydell ring any bells?"

"Lord have mercy!" Bernice exclaimed. "You mean he's from that bunch?"

"Yep, and I almost forgot." Darci reached into her jeans pocket and took out some folded pages. "I meant to give you these before I started explaining." She handed them each a couple papers stapled together. "Because I want bragging rights."

Mabel, done with the planting and now sitting beside her friend on the bench, elbowed Bernice. "We've gone and made . . . the girl a braggart."

"Better look out Darci, ain't no tellin' what you'll be by the time we get done with you." Bernice laughed. Darci was glad these ladies had grown so close to her over the past year.

"It's a copy of the original marriage bond from Missouri." The ladies shifted their papers to get a better look. "Shows he married Betsy Hicks at the justice of the peace's office in 1904, just like what Betsy's family bible had listed, only with his real name there, of course."

"I see," said Mabel. "Don't you love how pretty . . . their old handwriting is? People just scribble anymore . . . seems like."

"Looks a lot better than my chicken scratch," Bernice added, nodding her head. "It is right pretty. Reminds me a little of my mama's writing."

"And down there, under each of the wedding party's names, it gives their parents and where they were born. Titus Clydell was born and raised here in Dixon, and I guess most of his descendants still carry on that tradition." Darci thought for a minute. "Wade said the Clydells have been in politics ever since the Civil War. Stetson showed him around his house before Wade started the remodel. He has a whole wall full of framed pictures from each generation, with plaques underneath to show their titles. Wade thinks this Titus person was a senator or some such. Guess holding public office runs in Stetson's family."

"Anybody with eyes and ears around these parts knows Stetson's running for State Rep again this year. He's got fliers up on every light post between here and Kingdom Come, and he's already campaigning on the radio and television set." Bernice didn't look all that thrilled about Webster County's star politician. Charlie won't hush about it either."

"Can't blame him for being proud of his boy," Mabel added. "Even if he is . . . obnoxious about it."

"I'm not sure if he's gonna share your excitement about this," Wade said to Darci as she got out of her Volkswagen Bug. "He said he'd be happy to meet with you and thinks this whole thing sounded interesting." He gave his wife a quick peck on the cheek, then shut the car door. "Course I only told him about you helping a friend trying to find out about her family tree, that y'all had been looking into her great-granddaddy, Ellis Clydell, to learn more about him. Didn't mention the part about her thinking the rest of his family ran Betsy out of town, possibly tried to kill her and her kids. Didn't exactly know how he'd react to that."

Tired from putting in a hard day of work at Petal Pushers after another sleepless night, Darci had driven straight to Wade's work site after re-potting a couple hundred of those heirloom tomato slips she was so proud of. The seedlings had grown to the size where they had to be transplanted from the little starter pods to the slightly larger three pack containers. Hoyt suggested she might want to set up at the farmers market, when the plants were a little bigger. She hadn't thought of that before, though she loved to shop for fresh produce there. The fresh corn in the summer and fall were her and Paxton's favorite, with kernels so soft, sweet, and juicy, you could eat them raw. There was a woman who sold fresh brown eggs, a couple with their own beehives who brought jars of honey, and a young blonde lady, a baby girl always on her hip, who made soy candles in every scent imaginable. Darci had gone to her after Hattie got a whiff of Miss Addie's distinctive perfume, a scent last put on by the ghost in physical form some seventy years ago. Charlotte covered by saying it was a new candle, and that they'd get one for Hattie. So a few weeks ago Darci'd gone to the lady to order a few amber, rose, and vanilla scented candles. She couldn't wait to give one to Hattie the next time she saw her, and thought lighting the others in the shop might be a nice tribute to Miss Addie.

Anyway, she liked Hoyt's idea and told him she'd give him a small raise if he'd take some potted vegetables and flowers, to give the farmer's market a try. She could use all the help she could get paying off those damn greenhouses.

"Well," Darci said, "gee, thanks so much for saving that bombshell for me. How do you think he'll be with the new info?"

"Just remember, he's awful proud of his heritage, the people he comes from. Try to be objective, you know," Wade suggested, "like you're reporting on the facts, so keep your opinions to yourself. We weren't there when whatever happened all those years ago, so you can't accuse his great-grandpa or whoever for a crime that might never have happened."

"You really think I'm going to go in and ask him to bare all the family skeletons?" Darci gave him a playful elbow in the ribs, but grinned at him.

"Do you remember that game called gossip?"

"Um, yeah, the one where you sit in a circle and the first person passes a message to the next person in line, and when the secret gets passed all the way around, that person says it out loud." Darci frowned. "What's that got to do with any of this?"

"Hon, you're playing the game, starting with a message that's been passed around to some extent for a century or so." Wade looked apologetic as he pointed this out. "You're gonna have to expect some of the details to be a little skewed."

"Okay, you're probably right. But you have to admit, you've got to be curious about what happened to leave Betsy a widow on the run."

"I'm just a little curious, not all nosy like my wife." Wade rang the doorbell.

Before she had a chance to make a witty comeback to Wade's comment, Darci heard footsteps approach the large oak door. The grandeur of the home, with its Doric columns and stately antiquity, made her visualize the person who'd open the door as an old fashioned maid or butler, dressed in black and white formal work attire, sure to curtsy as they took their leave after showing the guests into the parlor. She should have known better. While plenty of folks in the area hired domestic help, anybody who put on airs like that, making nannies and housekeepers wear silly outfits and curtsy, would've been the talk of the town, and not in a good way.

The knob turned, the door opened without even the teeniest squeak on its well-oiled hinges, but instead of a butler, there stood a man she recognized from being in the shop last fall to pick up Wade's estimate. Miss Addie seemed to take an instant dislike to this guy, something totally out of her character. Darci still wasn't sure if the paper cut the man got as soon as the cold spot had settled around them was due to the ghost or just bad luck, but she knew the way the door slammed itself shut after he left was pure Miss Addie.

"Come on in." Stetson Clydell held the door open and gestured them inside his lovely home.

"How're you doing today, Darci? I already know how Wade is, since he's been working his backside off all day right here." His smile was genuine, even if all his political promises were not.

"I'm fine," Darci said, "how are you?" Darci followed Stetson through a wide foyer and into the first room on their right, glad she didn't experience the same overwhelming dislike for him as she had last fall. Today he seemed perfectly cordial.

The entranceway was more elegant than she could have imagined, with its tile floors, high ceiling, and the dark antique woodwork that surrounded her on all sides. An Asian runner covered the floor under her feet, woven in beautiful hues of burgundy, green, and gold, with violet highlights throughout.

"I'm fine, thanks so much for asking." Stetson motioned for Darci and Wade to have a seat on the sofa in the living room while he took the leather recliner directly across from them. "To tell you the truth, you've got the best of my curiosity. From what your husband told me, I do believe you just might have some details about my family tree that I've yet to discover."

"My curiosity has been piqued too, or I probably wouldn't have spent so much time helping my new friends work to find answers." Darci smiled. "I sure do thank you for taking the time to talk to me about this. I know Betsy's family, who we believe to be your long lost cousins, appreciate it as well."

"I'd like to have a copy of their contact information, if you don't mind," Stetson said, leaning back and making himself comfortable. "After you share the information you've come across, before my imagination runs away from me."

"Ellen is the one who first contacted me." Darci held a paperclipped stack of paper out for him to take. "Shane is her brother, and Trisha's their first cousin. Their phone numbers, addresses, and emails are on the top page. They want to meet you and anybody from this side of their family, whether they ever figure out what happened to their great-grandfather or not. The connection is what they told me they really want, though they're pretty hungry for some answers too."

Stetson leafed through the pages, his eyes skimming through them with visible interest. "You say Ellis is who they think their ancestor is?"

"Yes. All the documentation is in that packet. They hired a genealogist and dug around a little themselves. There's a marriage bond between Ellis Milton Clydell and Betsy Hicks from 1904 that lists his father as Titus Clydell of Webster County, Kentucky. That would be your great-great-grandpa, right?"

"Yes, that's right." Stetson flipped to the copy of the bond.

"Hattie Delaney is on the contact page too. She's not related, but the one thing that ties all of us, the ones trying to find out what happened to Ellis, is Miss Addie Brown." Darci felt a burst of pride just mentioning her name. "My flower shop

used to be her home. I met Hattie and her husband when they came through town and wanted
to visit her late grandmother's home place, and
we've stayed in touch ever since then."

"Did she know the Hicks-McGee descendants?"
Stetson had had to check the pages for the alias
Betsy had used. "Though they'd be Clydells, in
actuality, I think."

"No, and yes. Sorry, I'm getting ahead of myself."

"She does that a lot," Wade said, which earned
him a grin from Stetson. Darci could tell they'd
developed a friendship since Wade had been
working his carpentry magic on the manor renovations.

Disregarding his remark, Darci explained,
"This is the coolest part, how sometimes fate
steps in. Ellen wrote a letter to Miss Addie's kin
and mailed it to the address she found on her
great-grandmother's correspondence from decades ago, which is how I got it at Petal Pushers."

"Huh, you don't say," Stetson said. Darci was
happy to see that he was intrigued. She needed
his help as Ellis' next of kin, since his dad wasn't
about to stop being crabby and talk about whatever he knew. "Like it was meant to be."

"The letter, there's a copy of that in your stuff,"
Darci paused to point to it, "explains how Betsy
dropped all this on her deathbed. Sorry, I'll back
myself up here again. Betsy told her family she
had to take the twins baby girls, only a few days
old at the time, and leave town to hide from . . .
um, whoever was trying to hurt them. Miss Addie

was the midwife who delivered Ella and Emma, and she helped them get away. Betsy never re-married, but raised her girls under the name McGee, in Pennsylvania."

"What was she running from, or who?" Stetson asked. The leather cushion squeaked when he shifted to a more comfortable position.

Darci didn't want to say his murderous family, so she chose her words carefully. "She passed before she could get to what Ellis' real name was, but said something about her late husband's kin trying to harm them or take the children away. Her family has no idea why she thought that, what happened to Ellis, or any of this. Oh, so it'll be less confusing when you look through the papers, let me tell you that she only referred to Ellis as L. S. McGee, even in the family bible, which kind of supports the fact she was scared to death of anyone finding out who he really was."

"Why, if she feared for her life and the lives of her children, did she decide to divulge this? I mean, I understand why she'd feel it was necessary to finally unload that big secret, especially when she was fixing to die, but did she think the threat was gone?"

"We believe she wanted to tell them before, but didn't know if the people who she viewed as a threat were still living. Her dying wish was for her girls and grandchildren to claim the inheritance she'd found out about, and for them to learn why she'd had to run and hide their heritage." Darci noticed a strange expression pass across Stetson's face at the mention of inheritance. This worried her a little. If he thought they were after his money, that would be a very bad thing.

"Hmmm," Stetson leaned forward, then rested his chin on his hand, his elbow propped on the armrest. She had his full undivided attention, she was sure. "They think Uncle Ellis left a will or trust fund, something like that?"

"That part's kind of cloudy. The way I understand it, Titus left a clause in a will about money he wanted to go to his son Ellis and his heirs. Now, Ellen and them are kind of confused, because if for some reason Betsy was afraid of Titus, it doesn't make any sense that the man would leave them anything." That same odd look was still on Stetson's face, and grew more pronounced. "They aren't expecting there to be anything left for them, obviously, especially after all this time. They just want to find out what happened to Betsy and Ellis all those years ago."

"This is all very interesting." He leafed through the stack of paper Darci'd given him, as if searching for something. "I don't see a copy of the will."

"We don't have one." Darci felt her eyebrow lift a little, and she caught herself fidgeting with a tassel on one of the couch pillows. Stetson knew something, he had to. He knew there was a will, and that weird expression, devoid of his political mask, showed he was either surprised or worried, she couldn't tell which. "They weren't sure whose will the inheritance was in, but figured it was Titus'. Trisha is planning to contact a lawyer friend of hers, to see how to go about finding a record of it. What can you tell me about Ellis?"

"Why don't I show you our old family bible." Stetson stood and walked toward the hall, asking them to follow. "You can copy down anything you'd like, of course, to give to the other researchers. Ellis was Titus' oldest child."

They walked through the beautiful hallway that split the first floor in half. The last door on the left opened into a room Darci instantly labeled as the library. She didn't think Stetson used this as his home office, since it didn't have that type of feel. A small keyhole desk faced one wall, but there were no filing cabinets, printer, or computer to be seen.

She could imagine curling up on one of the easy chairs near the window, book in hand, for hours. The wooden floors, polished to a nice shine, held scars from years of use. Just last week Wade had mentioned how much he appreciated the fact Clydell Manor was still maintained that way, wearing the proud badge of its age, since it stood through the Civil War and many generations of Webster County history. It turned Wade's stomach to mush when other homeowners hired him to either cover floors like this with wall to wall carpeting or, worse yet, sanding the whole thing down to apply a new modernized finish; he'd come down with a sick headache after the Johnsons had him use glue and carpet staples to install gaudy blue shag over the original maple flooring in their home last summer.

An elegant dark green area rug lay angled in the sitting area in the center of the room. A library table stood in front of one wall, a matching antique chair at each end, and she would bet the single drawer in the middle was well stocked with paper, pens, and pencils to jot down references from the many books that filled the abundant shelves. She saw a large section of what she would call law books, and guessed it would be necessary for people in politics to stay well versed on laws in the state, as well as those legal terms that made her head hurt when she watched complicated crime movies. She was drawn more to the double shelves on the largest wall, filled with classic literature, mostly from Southern writers including Margaret Mitchell, Mark Twin, Truman Capote, William Faulkner, Harper Lee, Flannery O'Connor, Ernest Gaines, Cormac McCarthy, Tennessee Williams, and Kate Chopin. Another massive bookcase held biographies and autobiographies, including people from every continent and time period: Napoleon, Thomas Jefferson, Robert E. Lee, Alexander the Great, Charlemagne, George Washington, Ben Franklin, but also movie stars, athletes, and politicians from both parties, with a book on Ronald Reagan right next to hardbacks on both George Bushes.

The reference section near the table probably saw quite a bit of use, especially when the Clydell children were in school doing their homework. Dictionaries, a thesaurus, atlases and the like were located near an ornate globe, one that looked too old to have the latest updates but too elegant to update.

The wall of portraits Wade had told her about stood directly in front of them. Stetson proudly pointed out the men he descended from, emphasizing the political offices they'd each held. Hard to miss, since they were engraved on plaques underneath the frames. One picture drew Darci's attention.

"You are the spitting image of him," Darci said, taking a step closer to examine the resemblance in the photograph. "He's your grandpa, right?" The plaque underneath bragged that Terrence Elvin Clydell was once a congressman. Hairstyles aside, they looked exactly alike.

"Yes, and I always take it as a compliment when people say I look like Granddad." A genuine grin lit Stetson's face. "My oldest son has his jawline and our eyes."

Could that be the reason the ghost acted up when Stetson stopped by the shop? The idea about Miss Addie thinking Stetson was Terrence flitted through her mind, along with Hattie mentioning her grandmother's hatred for the whole family, but then her attention shifted to the records she needed to copy down.

The Clydell family bible held a place of honor behind a glass window in one of the bookcases. It had to be at least as old as the house, which Titus had built right before the Civil War. The leather binding showed slight signs of wear, but it was a museum quality tome. As Stetson took it out and tenderly placed it on the desk, Darci fought to restrain herself from fidgeting with the cover, to feel the embossed hundred-and-fifty-year-old leather under her fingertips. She crossed her arms behind her back, and caught Wade grinning at her, reading her mind.

Stetson opened the bible to its ribbon bookmark at a special section located between the old and new testaments for recording marriages, births, and deaths for many generations. She saw Titus' birth entry under his parents' names and wedding dates, then his marriage to Camilla, and under that, the names of their two boys. The oldest was Ellis Milton Clydell, born in 1883, but that was all. The slot for marriage was still blank, and the place for date of death contained only one small scribbled oval, as if someone had once started to write a word, managed only one or two letters, then decided to obliterate the record. No children were listed. Darci's heart melted at the sight of the vast emptiness that should have listed Ella and Emma, their mother Betsy, and all their grandchildren. She wondered if Stetson might add them himself, after he met with Ellen and her family.

Terrence was Titus and Camilla's sole heir after Ellis vanished from existence. Under Terrence were lines filled with his wife's name, their marriage date, and their three children. Charles James Clydell must be Stetson's cantankerous old daddy, better known to Darci as Charlie from Golden Days Retirement Home.

"How come there isn't anything for Ellis? His wife, death date, place of burial, why is everything still blank?" Darci asked.

This was just as weird as Betsy listing his alias in her family bible. With stuff like this going on, she didn't understand how anybody ever managed to pull their family trees together at all. Exactly what kind of skeletons were hiding in Clydell Manor's many closets she had no idea, but now she had to find out.

"He would have been long dead before I was a twinkle in my daddy's eye," Stetson said. Darci detected a bit of his political persona taking over. "I heard a few family stories of Uncle Ellis and my grandpa when they were boys, but nobody seemed to know where he went when he left town."

"What do you mean?" Darci hadn't expected him to say that, though not much at this point should surprise her.

"Well, story goes that Uncle Ellis had a big falling out with his Pappy, which is what they all called Pappy Titus. 'Bout all I know is Daddy said Uncle Ellis was supposed to have been running around with some wild woman Pappy thought wasn't fit to associate with. They had it out, Ellis up and moved away, and the two never spoke again." Darci had already jotted down the pertinent data, so Stetson closed the book, picked it up, then turned to replace it on its special shelf behind the protective glass door.

"Didn't he ever contact his mama or little brother? I can understand a family feud with Titus, but it looks like he'd have wanted to keep in contact with somebody." Darci tried not to look as intent on studying Stetson's expression as she actually was. She was pretty sure Wade noticed.

Stetson shook his head. "Not as far as I know. Titus was widowed years before all that went down."

"Betsy said Ellis died when the girls were three days old, but you don't think that's the case?" Darci tried to sound like the comment was off the cuff, not like she was accusing the Clydells of covering something up.

"This is the first I've heard of a wife and twins or Uncle Ellis dying young. It was so many years ago, I doubt any of us will ever know for certain." Stetson didn't seem to be lying, but his manner felt a little guarded. "The story I heard says he ran off."

"Was there any speculation about where he went? Like did he stay in the state, or possibly move out of the country, join the army, work the railroad, any little suggestion of what he might have done or where he might have gone, if he didn't die like Betsy thought?" Darci doubted he had an answer, but she had to ask.

"Sorry, but I have not the slightest clue." Stetson shook his head, then shrugged his shoulders.

"So I don't guess you have any idea as to where we should look for burial records?" Darci asked, hoping but already knowing the answer would be negative.

"He's not in the family plot, but that's the only thing I seem to know for sure. The Clydell cemetery is about a mile in back of the house." He pointed to the rear wall. "I've been there so many times, I could almost name the headstone inscriptions with my eyes shut. Some of the markers, the older ones, are really beautiful. Titus'

148

mother is buried in the center, with a carved marble angel beside her headstone that stands a little over five feet tall. Please tell Ellen to let me know when she'll be in town. I'd love to show it to her, and the house as well."

Stetson walked them to the front entranceway, which signaled that their meeting was at an end.

"I'm sure she and her family would love that. Thanks so much for taking the time to talk to me about this today. I really appreciate it." Darci had only picked up a few tiny tidbits she didn't already know, but anything new brought them that much closer to finding the truth.

"Thank you for letting me know that we possibly have another branch on our family tree." His statement led Darci to believe he wasn't a hundred percent convinced Betsy's information was accurate, even though he wouldn't have offered to open his home to them and show them the cemetery if he thought they were making things up.

Stetson flashed a big smile, only half full of politics, as he opened the massive front door for them. "Please keep me in the loop, no matter what y'all find out." He reached into his back pocket for his billfold, then handed Darci his card. "My email's on there, if you come across anything else. I look forward to adding anything you can find to document Ellis and Betsy's life and legacy to the genealogical files."

"Sure thing." Darci put his card in her purse.

"See ya tomorrow, Wade," he said as she and Wade made their way down the front steps. "My wife is bragging about all the work you're doing to all her lady friends. That's a pretty competitive bunch, so I have to warn you there's already talk a few of them want to hire you to outdo the others. You may have a closet war on your hands."

Miss Addie's Corncob Jelly

Makes about 4 or 5 half pint jars

My good friend Hattie Delaney was sweet enough to share this recipe with me, and I thought I'd share it this month. She found it in her grandmother's cookbook (that's Mrs. Addie Brown, who used to live in the house where Petal Pushers is located.) Some folks think this tastes like apple jelly, some say it tastes like honey, but everybody agrees that it's yummy.

You'll notice two versions here, one made from fresh corn on the cob and the other using dried red cobs, which you'd find in the field after the farmers harvest the crop with the combine. The dried red cobs make a prettier red

dish colored jelly, but the yellowish version from fresh cobs tastes about the same. Hattie gave me a jar she'd made, and it didn't last long. It is delicious.

Pay attention to whichever recipe you use, since cooking time and the amount of sugar are quite different in each.

The Dried Red Field Corncob Version

Ingredients:
12 corncobs found in the field after the combine leaves
7 cups water
3 cups sugar
1 package powdered fruit pectin

Cover the corncobs with the water in a large kettle or stock pot and boil for about thirty minutes. Remove from heat, cool, toss out the corncobs and strain the liquid through cheesecloth.

You'll need three cups, so add a little water to it if you need to.

Add the fruit pectin to this liquid and bring to a full rolling boil, then add the sugar and continue to boil it for three more minutes.

Take off the stove, skim off the foam, and pour into warm half pint jelly jars and seal.

The Fresh Corn Version

Ingredients:
12 fresh corncobs, with the kernels cut off and used in another recipe or frozen
4 cups water
4 cups sugar
1 package powdered fruit pectin

Cover the corncobs with the water in a large kettle or stock pot and boil for fifteen minutes.

Remove from heat, cool, throw away the cobs and strain the liquid through cheesecloth.

You'll need three cups, so add a little water to it if needed.

Return to the pot, stir in the pectin, and bring to a full rolling boil, add the sugar and boil for one more minute.

Remove from heat, skim any foam off, and pour into hot half pint jelly jars and seal.

Chapter Eight

The garden is the poor man's apothecary.
~ German Proverb

Darci sent Paxton upstairs. The boy was bored, so he'd tried to wait on a customer when a lady came in while Darci was in the bathroom. She liked his initiative and the pride he took in helping her out in the shop, but the ten-year-old was not well equipped to handle store business on his own, and from today's performance, wouldn't be for some years to come.

"He said what!?" Charlotte asked later that afternoon when she came in for the afternoon shift. As Darci told her the story, she laughed so hard her mascara smeared in raccoon smudges under her eyes.

The woman Paxton waited on told him, when he asked how he could help her, that she was in to pick out flowers for her friend's funeral. Paxton had never been to a funeral in his life, which left him ill prepared for the situation. He'd watched the others take down enough orders that it was easy for him to mimick what they usually did. He took the form from the counter, filled in the woman's name, address, and phone number, then signed his own name on the bottom just like Darci and Charlotte did. Darci showed it to Charlotte to prove she wasn't making the story up. She doubted the woman would ever return.

"When I came out of the bathroom, Kathy Hutchens stood sobbing by the counter. Paxton was near tears himself, but stood plucking Kleenex one after the other from the box, handing them to his first customer. I knew right away it was a bad situation, even before I asked what was the matter."

Paxton, bless his heart, had tried his best.

Kathy wanted to send a funerary wreath to be placed next to the casket. Her wording of it is what confused Paxton, who only had funerals from movies and television to use as a mental reference. He'd written on the order pad to include yellow roses and have something lavender on there, a ribbon or some such, since lavender was her favorite color.

"Then he asked me . . ." Kathy had sniveled, choking up even more. Paxton was practically throwing Kleenex at the woman by that point, his bottom lip trembling from the horror of the situation he found himself in. "He . . . wanted to confirm . . . where . . . I . . . wanted the wreath . . .plaaaaaced." She totally lost it again then.

"Do you want a glass of water?" Darci had

156

asked, dreading to find out what Paxton did to send the woman into hysterics.

"No, I'm going to leave now." Kathy took another handful of tissues from Paxton and backed toward the door, still sobbing. She extended her hand toward Paxton. "Know you didn't mean it . . . it's okay." She glanced at Darci through her tears. "Cancel," she paused to sniffled and blew her nose with a honk, "the order."

The door bells jingled behind one customer Darci knew she could kiss goodbye forever.

"Oh my God, Pax," Darci said, staring at her son, a blizzard of tissue around his feet, his bottom lip quivering. "What in the world did you do, son?"

She'd taken the slip from him then, saw the order, and noticed he'd underlined his note of placing the wreath beside the casket. Okay, so she still had no idea what had caused Kathy Hutchens that degree of distress. At least she was polite to her son, even while that upset, which made Darci think that perhaps she had a child of her own.

"I didn't mean to hurt her feelings, Mom," Paxton said, his eyes wide and sad. Darci's heart broke just looking at her little boy. "I don't even know why she got so upset. I was just trying to fill in while you took a whiz."

"I know, Pax, everything's fine. I'm not mad, but I need to know what made her cry. Next time you want to help, make sure one of us adults are in the room, or you can tell a customer to wait just one second until one of us comes back, and just casually keep them company until then. Okay?"

"Okay, but I was just tryin' to help."

"What, exactly, did you say right before she broke down in tears?" Darci kept her voice calm to to show Paxton she wasn't mad. "She mentioned something about you confirming where she wanted the funeral wreath placed. What did you say?"

"I just wanted to conbirm where she wanted it. See, I wrote down what flowers she wanted and everything." Paxton pointed at the order pad.

"You mean 'confirm', and yep, you did fill this out right. Let's get back to what your exact words were."

"I wanted to make sure I had her stuff right, so I read it back to her." Paxton took a deep breath, a handful of tissues still in his fisted hand. "She said she wanted the wreath beside the casket, so I asked if she meant down in the hole. Then she started bawling, so I said, sure, we can put the wreath in the hole, we'll just pitch it right down in there after they dump the coffin in."

"Um, Pax," Darci started, but she couldn't begin to find the right words. She sighed and gave him a hug. "We'll talk through this later, but for now, just let me say people are very sensitive when they their loved ones die, so we have to be very, very careful how we phrase things. But we'll go over that later. For now, why don't you go find something constructive to do upstairs."

Darci needs some sleep, poor girl. I know just the thing to do the trick too, so she can get some rest. Just might help me put a few other ideas in her head too.

Thing is, I do believe I might have to call in a favor to get my plan to work. Betsy always was better at this kind of thing, sleep and dreamin' and such. Now let me see, which one of those books covers mugwort?

"Darce, you know I love ya." Charlotte handed her a fresh cup of coffee, spiked with plenty of sugar. "But you look like warmed over cat poo this morning."

"Thanks," Darci said as she took a sip. "For the coffee, not the insult, even though I do feel like something that crawled out of a litter box."

"Still can't sleep, huh?" Charlotte leaned against the counter as Darci shook her head. "I know how miserable that is, thanks to Cole during his phase of wanting to get up to play and eat every fifteen minutes before he started sleeping through the night. You're gonna have to get a grip before you make yourself sick."

"When I do fall asleep, I wake up every hour or so with the nervous shakes, worrying about getting everything done and paying off the greenhouses." Darci ran her fingers through the hair she'd barely bothered to brush. She made a mental note to call Donovan for an appointment the first chance she got, because the last thing she needed was to send her customers screaming out of the shop, thinking a scarecrow came to life to wait on them. "Any little noise wakes me up, and before I know it, I'm standing by the front door in my slippers, half dreaming that some other catastrophe hit the shop."

"I'd hoped you would relax a little, now that you have the class thing figured out. You've got what, seven people signed up already?"

"Nine as of this morning. Maybe I can sleep an hour before the first class next week. Can't fall asleep during a demo and have the students drop out because I'm a screw up." Darci groaned. "Great, I guess that'll be on my nightmare rotation now, right between the one with an elephant busting into the shop through the side wall and the one where a tornado yanks Petal Pushers off the ground and leaves me standing there in the freezing rain holding a lightning rod. All I can do is stare up at the shop spinning away as I listen to the door bells jingle through the wind, rain, and thunder. Freddy Krueger would be a welcome sight compared to all that."

"You need to take some sleeping pills or something," Charlotte suggested.

"Tried that. Didn't help much and made me even groggier the next morning. Counting sheep and hot milk don't work either." Darci covered a yawn with her hand. "The milk made me want to get back up to make cookies."

Charlotte walked behind the counter to peruse the book shelves. "Let's find you an herbal remedy." She sat beside Darci with a thick book on the subject. "Hmmmm, that's weird. It opened right up to a page on insomnia."

"Chamomile isn't strong enough," Darci said as she ran her finger over the page so her sleepy eyes wouldn't lose their place. "Magnolia bark, valerian, passion flower, mugwort-"

They both looked toward the front of the shop when the bells on the door jingled. No one was there, and the door was still shut.

"Me thinks Miss Addie is voting for, what was the last one?" Darci waited for a reply, from the human beside her as well as the one who'd passed on in 1941. The bells remained still, but the parakeet went into the usual tweeting frenzy she used to greet the ghost.

"Mugwort," Charlotte said, then rubbed her suddenly chilled arms. "Guess the cold spot is her seal of approval."

"It says one option is to put the plant under my pillow to induce sleep, but that's out of the question. Mugwort grows wild but I don't trust myself to tell it and ragweed apart, since they look about the same. Wade's allergic to it so the mugwort would probably make him sneeze and wheeze just as bad."

"It comes in a tea," Charlotte said as they both read the next paragraph.

"Oh, lucky me. Bitter and acrid doesn't quite sound delicious." Darci wrinkled up her nose and stuck out her tongue.

"That leaves the mugwort capsules." Charlotte swiveled around to grab the phone. "Bet the health food place at the mall carries it."

When she hung up, a bottle of mugwort was on hold for Hoyt to pick up on his way to work. Charlotte texted him with the details, and hoped he wouldn't forget.

One June morning Darci pulled up to Golden Days Retirement Home, cheerful as ever. It was a beautiful day, with a robin's egg blue sky, white fluffy cotton candy clouds, everything green with summer growth. Sparrows sang a song as Darci unloaded the wheelbarrow from the back, set five red geraniums inside, ivy dangling over the edge of each pot, and shut the door. She smiled as she walked past the Confederate jasmine she'd planted outside Mabel's window to surprise her; she'd never forget the way Mabel Guthrie's face lit up when she saw it the next morning. Since she came at this time each week, she'd bet her bottom dollar Bernice and Mabel were watching out the window, waiting for her to pull up.

Sure enough, as soon as she'd picked up the first flower pot her two friends stepped through the back door. They joined Darci on the patio, exchanged small talk and asked how she was doing.

"Relieved. I was dreading getting down on my knees to weed around those roses out front." Darci winked in their direction. "Looks like I had a helper beat me to it. Sure do appreciate it, Mabel."

Mabel had a habit of pulling weeds, dead heading rosebushes and flowers, anything she could do outdoors to help. She'd been an avid hobby gardener all her life, and when she started sneaking out early in the mornings to take care of the landscape, it changed her life. She'd crawled out of her shell, made friends at the retirement home, and her health had drastically improved.

"You know I love . . . gettin' my hands dirty." Mabel grinned at her. She sat down on the bench, her cane hooked on the armrest. She didn't have to use it as much as she once did, and sometimes Darci thought she carried it as a security blanket.

Bernice propped her flip-flop clad feet up on the wheelbarrow, then crossed her ankles. She wore her straw hat today, and her face seemed to beam even brighter than the summer sunshine. "Gretta Carmichael told me that husband of yours is putting in the king daddy of all closets over at Clydell Manor. Motorized shoe organizers, a walk-in big enough to host Thanksgiving dinner with about twenty guests. How much is that moron paying for all that mess?"

"Uh, I don't really know." Darci honestly didn't. Wade was being paid well for his work, but he didn't usually mention what each job brought in. He was more into talking about the details, the wood he worked with, the design, and old school craftsmanship. "But I did see some hellacious sketches, and I'm jealous."

"Motorized shoe shelves?" Mabel shook her head.

"Kind of like one of the contraptions that rotate to keep hot dogs warm," Bernice said. "Right Darci?"

"That's a pretty good way to describe it. Did Gretta tell you what the racks look like? They have-"

"Is that you, Darci Shelton?" A large heavyset old man came stomping toward her, a scowl on his face, hands clenching and unclenching. He wasn't there to celebrate joining the local welcome wagon, that was for sure.

"Well, is that your name?" he bellowed even louder. Whoever this man was, he reminded Darci of a big fat locomotive coming at her full speed, and she could clearly imagine steam pouring out of his ears.

"Uh . . ." Darci knew if Max saw her right now, with the expression she felt take shape on her face, he'd say her eyes were as big around as mule turds, something he'd said to her quite a few times as she was growing up. She looked back at her friends. Both had stood up and were stepping toward her. Mabel looked disgusted at the loudmouth but also like he worried her a little. Bernice bounded in front of her to keep the man from getting into Darci's face.

"What do you mean, charging up to a complete stranger, screaming your fool head off?" Bernice put a hand on her hip and pointed her finger at the man whose expression made Darci wonder if he'd been sucking on a lemon after it had rolled through a fresh pile of cow poop. "What in the world's the matter with you, you old fart?"

The old fart trudged forward until there was only a foot between himself and Bernice. Her wagging forefinger filled most of that gap. Bernice was fearless, but Darci was afraid this guy might actually start swinging punches. He was royally pissed about something or other. If she'd known this was going to happen, she would have brought Hoyt along as a bodyguard.

"Ain't nothing the matter with me, *Bernice*." He'd said her name in a mock whinny voice, which went along with the sour expression on his face as he tipped his big head from side to side. He looked like a geriatric Baby Huey. "Get that finger out of my face or I'm gonna bite it clean off your hand." He tried to sidestep around her, but the more agile Bernice continued to block his path to Darci.

Mabel moved to stand shoulder to shoulder with Bernice, her cane held lengthwise in front of her, her weaker left hand shaking under the weight on her palm. Bernice nodded her approval. Darci figured she'd better do something to stop this before somebody got hurt. She realized she'd just stood there the whole time with her mouth hanging open.

"Can I help you?" Darci put herself between and just slightly behind those of her cane barricaded buddies. "You hollered my name when you rounded the building."

"That's what I thought," he practically snorted. "Come back to poke your nose in everybody's b'ness again. You best attend to your own backyard and leave other folks alone."

"Afraid poking around in other people's yards is my job."

"You know full well what I'm talking about, girly." He put his hands on his hips and frowned even harder.

"I really don't even know who you are or what you're so mad about," Darci said, wondering what the hell she'd done to tick this old dude off.

"You been stirring up the stink, that's what I'm so POed about. If I was still the mayor-"

"This old fart is Charlie Clydell." Bernice stuck her palm toward the man in a tell it to the hand gesture to interrupt his tirade. She glanced over her shoulder at Darci. "Remember, I told you how ornery he was." She looked back at Charlie. "I wasn't lying."

"Mr. Clydell, what is it that's irritating you so much?" Darci noted the perspiration dotting his forehead and his heavy breathing. She hadn't done anything to deserve his screaming fit, but she'd never forgive herself if he dropped dead in front of her. "Maybe you'd like to have a seat over in the shade and we can talk about whatever's bothering you."

"Don't need to sit down!" Charlie might just blow his vocal chords, if he kept on yelling like that. "My son mentioned you were over to the house, being all nosy 'bout stuff that don't concern you. I want you to mind your own b'ness!"

"Stetson was as nice as he could be, and offered to show some of my friends around his estate the next time they're in town. I find it hard to believe he told you I was doing anything to upset him. All I did was-"

"Oh, I know exactly what you're up to. You got Lucy and Ethel here to bug the residents, asking 'em what the Clydells did way back when to send Uncle Ellis out of the county for good. Heard *Bernice—*" again, Charlie whined out her name as he made a sour prissy face. Bernice just huffed at him. "—ask Mary Stevens if she'd heard tell of an Indian woman with twin half breed brats having to get out of town fast, a hundred years ago. Why would you give a damn about some century old Injuns, anyway?"

"Charlie Clydell, you big fat moron." Bernice shook her finger as she spoke. Mabel twirled her cane around as if to remind him she still held it, in case she should have to rough him up a bit. "You know better than to talk to a lady that way. She ain't hurt a thing."

"She's trying to start up rumors to ruin my boy's chances in the election this comin' fall, is what she's hurting." He tugged his belted waistband up over his potbelly.

"Where is your Uncle Ellis, Mr. Clydell?" This old guy would probably never want to speak to Darci again, she hoped, except maybe to yell at her some more. She couldn't pass up the chance to ask him something important while she could. "His great-grandkids are trying to find out where he went and where his final resting place is."

"Don't know where he is and wouldn't tell you even if I did and had a picture postcard with his stupid face on it!" Charlie screamed. He pulled a handkerchief from his pocket and mopped the sweat off his forehead. The veins in his neck bulged to the point Darci could nearly see them pulsate.

Not surprisingly, one of the staff nurses heard the commotion and trotted around through the back door onto the patio. She appeared worried when she saw Charlie's condition. "What's going on out here?"

"This old idiot is pickin' on Darci, working hisself into a tizzy," Bernice said. She and Mabel crossed their arms and glared at Charlie.

"He's keeping her . . . from her work," Mabel added. "Should be ashamed of himself."

"Screaming like a banshee at poor Darci." Bernice shook her head in disgust.

"Mr. Clydell, you don't need to get yourself all worked up like this." The nurse took Charlie's arm and tried to lead him back inside the building. "Let's go get you a nice glass of lemonade and one of your pills-"

"Not til *she* leaves." Charlie pointed at Darci. "And quits pokin' her big nose into everything. That girl is harassing my entire family, even the ones long dead!"

"Let's let her get back to tending the landscape, and get you inside and calmed down."

He gave Darci the stink eye, tried to holler something else at her, and took to coughing. The nurse patted him on the back, then took his pulse.

Darci wondered why the nurse seemed to believe Bernice rather than Charlie's claim she was harassing him. Maybe it was due to the man's crabby character, which Bernice had described on the phone a few weeks ago. Or maybe it was because Charlie was chewing the three of them out when the nurse got to him. Either way, she was glad to see her drag him through the door, away from them.

That man was in dire need of a sedative and an anger management class.

Darci flipped through a magazine a few days later. The beautiful landscape on one page caught her eye, and she allowed herself a moment to daydream. An ancient castle stood in a field of green. Well, it must have been lawn, but that was one hell of a yard and she was personally glad her behind didn't have to mow it. She'd give her eye teeth to sink her hands into the borders and the formal knot garden pictured on the following page. The place called to her mind every childhood fairy tale she'd ever wanted to make a guest appearance in.

If she could magically make that her world, what would her title be? Queen Darci? The Dutchess of Daffodils? Hoyt walked in just then, which brought her back to rural Kentucky, far away from castles and aristocracies. She'd have been Dame Darci, Boss Lady of the Bulbs, if her favorite delivery boy had anything to do with it.

"Hey Hoyt, how's it going?" A list of deliveries awaited him on the counter. Darci handed it to him as they talked, then he trotted off to the workroom to pick up the orders he needed to load into the van.

"Well, what do you know," Darci said to Daisy as the parakeet nibbled on a fresh sprig of millet. "He actually didn't say it for once. Ha!"

But then Hoyt returned to the room to ask about the number on one of the addresses. "Couldn't tell if this was supposed to be fifteen or sixteen, but wanted to check before I went to the wrong door, gave the wrong lady a present, then had to pry it out of her hands." He winked at her.

"That's a sixteen, the Adams' place." She told him to drive carefully, below the speed limit. The ticket he got last month—which Max managed to 'fix' so Hoyt didn't lose any points on his license—gave her a good reason to remind him.

"Sure thing, Boss Lady." Hoyt's earbud's went into his ears.

"Way worse things he could be calling me, I guess." Magazine in hand, she flipped through a few more pages until Max dropped by Petal Pushers for an unexpected visit.

Darci was happy to see him, as always, but his expression suggested something was on his mind other than browsing through flower petals.

"Charlotte, if you've got things covered up here, I need to get some coffee brewing for my favorite cop."

Max grinned sheepishly as he followed her to the kitchen. He got them each a mug from the cabinet over the sink, and a spoon apiece from the cutlery drawer, then took his usual seat at the table. Darci poured water in the coffee maker, then leaned against the counter as she waited for it to brew.

"So, to what do I owe this surprise visit? You don't seem to be bubbling over with good news and tidings of joy, so what's up?" The coffeepot started whizzing out the java, and the aroma took over the kitchen.

"I just need to talk to you for a sec, but not til I get my free cup of joe." He made small talk with Darci until then.

Wondering what her godfather was about to tell her, in his capacity of sheriff, made her nerves act up. Her left hand fidgeted with the back of her earring, and she had the worst craving for chocolate covered custard filled Krispy Kreme donuts. Her stomach growled, though she'd eaten lunch just two hours before. The pot was full now, but Max still hadn't told her why he was there. He'd just asked how Paxton's curve ball was coming along, and if Wade was having any luck learning to make those new fly fishing lures they'd talked about.

Darci poured them both a steaming cup of coffee, filled the little china creamer shaped like a cow with milk, grabbed a package of Paxton's fudge-striped shortbread cookies—the generic, not the ones with the little elves on the front, since Darci was trying to save as much as possible to pay everything off—in lieu of the Krispy Kremes she didn't buy because she'd gained back five of the eleven pounds she'd lost. She took the seat beside Max, who took an inordinate interest in tracing the fudge stripes with his pinky finger.

171

"Okay, Max." Darci spooned sugar into her cup and then passed the china sugar bowl to him. "Tell me what's up. You and Mae alright?"

Her mind always flew to health at the first sign of anything being wrong. Paxton's sniffle, Wade's cough, her mother's migraine headaches, Charlotte's fatigue since Cole was born, and baby Cole wincing, coughing or sneezing while in her care all made her worry something worse could happen. She was no psychologist, but common sense and a little late night internet surfing pointed to the fear being due to her father dying unexpectedly when she was thirteen. He had drowned, but the sudden death by accident, the turmoil she felt then and still to some extent to this day, fueled the fear of losing her loved ones.

"We're just fine Darci, my little worry wart, it's nothin' like that." Max stirred milk into his cup. "It's just some minor official business, concerning you, that we need to discuss. Nothing major, so don't go hyperventilating or anything."

Darci had no idea what legal matter he could possibly need to speak to her about, but then she remembered something.

"Oh, man. Don't tell me Hoyt went and got another speeding ticket in the delivery van. I told that boy to keep his foot off the accelerator." She'd just have to go and order one of those thingies she'd seen on tv, a device that made the vehicle shut down if it went more than six miles an hour over the speed limit. The Boss Lady would so put a stop to Hoyt the speed demon.

"No, he hasn't got any more tickets, at least

not that I know about." Max didn't look at her, which meant he dreaded whatever was to come next. She'd known him since before she could crawl and was well versed in his body language.

"That, at least, is a relief." Darci's shoulders relaxed. "So what is it? Come on, it's not like you to beat around the bush."

Max reached into his pocket and pulled out an official looking document. He slapped it against the table a few times, deep in thought, before he spoke. "I have to deliver this to you, Darci. It's a restraining order."

"A what?!" Darci felt her forehead crinkle up in surprise. Now she'd need to order some of the anti-wrinkle cream she saw on that late night infomercial. "Who? What on earth would possess anybody to get a restraining order on me?"

Max handed her the paper, but at least he didn't say 'you've been served' like in the cop shows on TV.

"Charlie Clydell. He's a jackass and everybody knows it, but he had his lawyer file this."

"Why would he do this? I mean, he had a little hissy fit last week, but I didn't do anything to him. I'd never even met the lunatic before he came barreling around Golden Days Retirement Home screaming at me to mind my 'b'ness', as he put it." Darci felt like she needed to puke. Instead, she reached for another cookie and chomped away.

"He claims you're harassing him and his family, that you're trying to cast aspersions against his son to keep him from getting elected as state representative." Max looked her in the eye and she could tell he knew Charlie Clydell was full of shit.

A cold spot settled in the room. Miss Addie was apparently upset by the news as well.

Darci jumped when she saw the creamer hurl itself off the table. The crash that followed echoed off the walls.

The parakeet's frantic tweets let Darci know she hadn't imagined what she'd just seen.

"Sorry, Darci, must've hit it with my elbow. Somehow or other." Max bent to pick up the broken china that used to be shaped like a cow, until it had smashed on the floor hard enough to shatter into at least a hundred pieces.

I know what Clydell pulled last time he said those words, and now he's a-threatenin' Darci! Lord help me, I cain't let him hurt anybody else, especially not my Darci girl! He'll have to go through me get to her.

My head's poundin' again, and that same ole rage is a-churning in my stomach. I'm so upset, I don't know what to do with myself.

After they cleaned up the spilled milk and broken china, Darci read over the document Max had handed her.

"Oh no, Max, he can't do this to me. This says I can't go within a hundred feet of him." She continued to skim through the legal rigmarole, then, startled, her eyes darted to Max, almost pleading for help. "This says the restraining order is also in effect for everyone who's helped us research Ellis and Betsy. It lists Bernice and Mabel by name. He can't do this, can he? You won't make those two fine ladies move because of him? This is all my fault, I'm such an idiot. All I wanted to do was help Ellen and her family, and it was fun, I'm not gonna lie, but Charlie can't do this."

"Yes, he can, but I'm ahead of you on the rest of it." Max took a swig of coffee before the cup clinked gently against its saucer.

"What do you mean?" Darci shoved another cookie into her mouth, then fidgeted with the crumbs on the table in front of her.

"I called his attorney and got him to amend the thing so Bernice and Mabel can continue to live in the same building as that peckerwood. Had to talk to Vera Thompkins too, but everything will be fine. They just can't speak to Charlie, not that they'd want to now anyhow.'"

"Oh, I bet Bernice wants to give him a good talkin' to about now." Darci could not believe this was happening.

"That I'd love to see, but she can't. Vera is gonna make sure they don't eat at the same time, and she's drawing up a chart to show when each of 'em can use the common areas. Don't worry your pretty little head about them."

Darci sighed. She would never sleep again if she thought she'd caused problems for either of those dear sweet ladies, the very ones who'd stepped in front of her to take the brunt of Charlie's wrath.

"Wait." She could barely wrap her mind around the thought that had just clouded her brain. "Oh, hell no."

"Everything's going to be fine, Darci. No need to panic." Max reached out to pat her hand.

"Golden Days is my biggest landscaping account. I can't stop working there, especially now with these extra bills. I just can't, Max. That would kill me!" Darci felt her lip quiver. They were the first long term contract she'd signed after opening for business. The building was located in the center of town, the perfect location to showcase her hard work. Nothing would be worse for Petal Pushers than losing that account.

"I got that under control too, Darci Doodle." That had been Max's pet name for Darci when she was in junior high. "Don't worry, I talked to the lawyer and Vera about this, and everything is still doable. Vera made out a schedule for the three parties that live at Golden Days Retirement Home, so they won't accidentally cross paths. She was totally on your side and had a few choice words for Charlie, let me tell you. Anyway, now you just need to schedule your trips to the retirement home before noon, which is when Vera thought you usually liked to visit anyway. She has Charlie penciled in to be in his room or in the downstairs recreation area during that slot on Tuesdays. See, everything is going to work out just fine."

"That man is hiding something." Darci was getting mad now. "Is it really that easy for somebody to get a restraining order?" She still couldn't believe this was happening. "If anything, he was the one threatening us, the way he hollered at me and got up in Bernice's face and carried on. We didn't do a dang thing to him."

"Well no, a restraining order isn't that hard to come by. Charlie called his lawyer and said y'all were starting rumors about his son that would ruin his chance in the election this November, and that you got Mabel and Bernice to harass him." Max frowned, looking none too happy as he took a long sip of his coffee.

"Great."

"The nurse from the home, when the lawyer talked to her, told him she was afraid Charlie would have a heart attack or at the least get his blood pressure up too high. She didn't know who said what, though she did mention that Charlie had a bad temper." Max set his cup down. "Said he was red faced, sweaty, and his pulse was racing after the incident."

"Yeah, he was, but that's because he was screaming himself sick, at me mostly." Darci's nerves flip-flopped around to the point where she didn't know whether to laugh, cry, or go throw up in the toilet. "Un-freaking-believable."

Petal Pushers Plant Profile for Mugwort

Artemisia vulgaris
Perennial

Mugwort is also called wormwood, felon's herb, chrysanthemum weed and St. John's plant.

Brief description: Mugwort looks so much like common ragweed, it's hard to tell them apart since both grow wild on the side of the road. For herbal use, it's best to buy mugwort sold as tea or in pill form, so you don't get a hold of the wrong thing.

Trivia: At one time, mugwort was used to flavor drinks and in beer making.

Growing instructions: Um, really, mugwort is a wild growing weed. It's easy to grow, but I seriously doubt you're going to want to plant it in your flower bed.

Herbal uses: Mugwort is a remedy for insomnia, and is used to induce vivid dreams. Mugwort is good for digestive disorders, expels worms from

the intestines, and helps relieve stress, headaches, muscle spasms and vomiting.

Chapter Nine

*My green thumb came only as a result of the
mistakes I made while learning to see things
from the plant's point of view.*
~ H. Fred Dale

Darci felt more relaxed sitting in Donovan's chair
at the Hair Dare Your 'Do Salon than she had in
weeks. She'd almost nodded off with her head in
the shampoo bowl as Donovan massaged her
scalp and rinsed conditioner down the drain.
He'd squeezed her in that morning, and she was
too tired to worry about being away from Petal
Pushers during business hours, something she
never liked to do. Her concentration lagged due to
the insomnia and made her clumsier than usual,
so she was glad Charlotte was at the shop holding things together as best she could.

"Sure you only want me to trim the ends?"
Donovan asked, his scissors at the ready.

"Yep." Darci saw disappointment flicker over

his face. "But next time I promise to let you try something new and daring. Well, not too extreme, but different anyway."

"Has your friend had any luck finding out what happened to her great-grandpa?" Donovan snipped away at her split ends.

"No, we haven't made much progress since Mrs. James verified Ellis Clydell's name with the marriage bond. I talked to Stetson about it, explained that Ellen wants to connect with her long lost family and all, but he didn't seem to know any more about it than we do." Darci fidgeted with the apron cape thingy that was supposed to keep hair from getting all over her. She'd been so absorbed in the problems at Petal Pushers lately, she hadn't spent much time working on the Betsy and Ellis enigma. Her fingers worked the hem on the purple waterproof fabric as guilt set in.

"What did he say about the part where his family tried to whack a widow and her two babies? Bet he won't bring that up in his campaign speeches." Donovan winked at her reflection in the mirror in front of them and snipped away.

"Didn't actually put it like that. He wasn't liable to tell me anything if I accused his ancestors of attempted murder. May have been my imagination, but I think he knows a little more than he let on." Darci caught his eye again. "Especially when I asked when Ellis died and where he's buried."

"Do you think they actually killed him? I mean Stetson wasn't alive then, obviously, but do you really think that if some old guy in his family offed Ellis, they'd brag about it over Sunday supper?"

"At this point, I have no idea. Charlie might. Okay, probably not, but I felt like he knows something he didn't want to tell me."

"OMG, wouldn't it be something if Wade tore into one of those walls in Clydell Manor and found a real live skeleton! Well, not alive, but can you imagine Stetson talking his way around that at his next press conference?" Donovan performed an impersonation of Stetson doing just that. They both laughed so hard they had to break out the Kleenex.

"Makes you wonder what clues are hidden in those stately old walls. I still think they'd have to have some idea what became of Ellis. Even if he did run off like Stetson said, there had to be a letter or telegram or something. Oh, it sure would be fun to snoop around in their attic, and in the dumpsters where Wade pitches the material they take out during construction."

"That sparkle in your eye makes me think you're up to something."

"Bradley's supposed to be at the Clydell place today, isn't he? I think Wade mentioned they had some details to iron out about the new additions." Darci twirled her hair around her finger.

Donovan tapped her pinky with his comb to remind her not to fidget with her hair mid 'do. "Yeah, Mrs. Clydell decided to move their bedroom window over about a foot, so the sun won't be in her eyes as early." He rolled his eyes, then tapped Darci's hand again when she fiddled with another honey brown lock.

"I hope you don't have any appointments scheduled after me," Darci said, tucking her hands under her legs to keep them still, "because we're going out to lunch."

About an hour later, Darci parked her green VW Bug beside the curb in front of Clydell Manor. She and Donovan giggled as they walked up to the front door, since both were itching to get a peek at the walk-in closet that was the talk of Webster County.

"I hope they haven't ate yet, and that they have time to go to the diner with us." Darci pressed the doorbell.

"We probably should've called first." Donovan adjusted his sunglasses. "But now maybe you'll get a chance to poke around like I know you're dying to do."

The housekeeper, dressed in jeans and a t-shirt, answered the door. They followed her to the study and found Bradley and Wade hunched over blueprints. When invited out to lunch, they both smirked. Wade reached in his pocket for a five dollar bill.

"You win," he said, handing the cash to Bradley.

"We should consider ourselves lucky they didn't scale up the side of the house and tweet pictures of the shoe rack." Bradley pocketed the fiver.

"What are you guys talking about? We just thought you'd be hungry," Donovan said.

"Uh-huh." Wade leaned back against the desk.

"My bet was on y'all coming sometime next week. So, I guess we'd better let you see that closet or you'll stop by later with milk and cookies."

"We have no idea what you're talking about," Darci said, attempting to look wide-eyed and innocent. She made a show of checking her watch. "I have to get back to the shop before one, but yep, I think we have just enough time to let you show us what you've been working on before we head to the diner."

"You want to check out the pool house first, or the pantry expansion?"

Bradley's offer made Donovan and Darci grimace in unison. Wade and Bradley laughed, then lead the way up the staircase.

"Don't even think about snapping any pictures with your cell," Bradley warned as he and Wade stood at the closed double doors to the closet.

"Or diving into the pile of shoe boxes in the corner," Wade added, pointing his comment at Darci.

"Okay, we promise to be on our best behavior, so can we please take a peek?" Darci begged.

"Pretty please," Donovan added.

Wade and Bradley opened the doors. Darci and Donovan entered the closet, eager to see all the gadgets they'd heard so much about. Wade and Bradley headed back to the study to put away the plans they'd been working on, after making them promise to be down in two minutes, or else.

Disappointed the revolving shoe rack wasn't finished yet, the two raved about the pink and black damask upholstery on the settee and chairs, which looked stunning against the smoky lilac walls. They were about to go back downstairs, had just closed the closet doors and entered the hallway, when they walked past the open door to the attic. Wade had mentioned spending part of the morning up there to reinforce the closet light fixtures he'd installed.

"Hey, you stand here, where you can see the stairs, and cough real loud if anybody heads this way," Darci whispered. "I would never forgive myself if I didn't at least glance up there."

"It's not like they're gonna have a box labeled Family Secrets." Donovan wasn't overjoyed about the idea. "Fine, I'll stand guard, but hurry up." He cast a worried glace toward the staircase. "And I want the recipe for that coconut cake you served the last time we had supper at your house."

"Deal." Darci raced up the attic steps on her tippytoes.

The attic was dark and musty, with midday light filtering in through two small windows. The stuff tucked away up there was pretty much what you'd find in any attic: old furniture, toys outgrown generations ago, holiday decorations, and boxes with miscellaneous crap crammed under the lids. Donovan was right. She had absolutely no idea what she was looking for, and probably wouldn't have found it even if she had. Still, she thought she ought to at least make a circuit through the room, just to see if anything caught her attention.

"Ouch," she muttered when her shin bumped

against a rusty fan with baskets piled on top of it. As she rubbed her leg, a mass of books stacked up on an old chair caught her eye. There was just enough light to make out the titles in the pile, which seemed to be outdated text books and novels so old the cracked spines barely held them together. A picture album jutted out near the bottom. She walked closer to the window with it, hoping a sunbeam might land on a clue long forgotten on one of its ancient yellowed pages.

The first page held scribbled writing too faint to decipher. She took another step toward the window to make the most of the dappled light. Her sandal collided with something, and the next thing she knew, she'd stumbled backward into a shadowy corner. Luckily, her butt made contact with the wall and kept her from falling all the way down, but she dropped the album.

Still stooped over, she reached to pick it up.

A spider crawled across her knuckles. Only a small squeak of a scream escaped before she stifled it, in the midst of slapping herself and jumping from one foot to the other, as if that would help, swatting at the spider's path up her arm until she fell backward again after banging into more junk.

She landed on her side, then something bulky fell on top of her. She struggled to sit up, pretty sure she'd knocked the damn spider off, and untangled herself from the clothes or blanket, whatever fabric she was nearly buried under. Some long thing weighed her down. She managed to scoot a couple feet along the floor, scattering old clothes in her wake. A rolled up area rug under some shirts was heavy, but she finally managed to push it off of herself.

Then something rolled out of it.

She screamed, and that time she didn't give one sweet damn who heard her.

Darci was halfway down the attic stairs when Donovan, running to see what was wrong, nearly crashed into her. That startled another scream out of her, which made Donovan yelp as well.

All she managed to say was, "Dead body! Ellis . . . up there!"

By now, everyone in the house had heard the commotion and scrambled to see what the heck was going on.

Wade bounded up to her side, Bradley close on his heels. "Darci, are you hurt?" His eyes scanned her for injury before he brushed her bangs to the side and touched the scar on her forehead, the one left from the shooting last fall. "What's going on?"

Donovan's arm wound around Darci, patting her shoulder. He guided her back, putting a few steps between them and the attic she'd just announced to be a crime scene. "Oh my gosh. She saw a body up there-"

"It fell on me," Darci interrupted, her heart racing a mile a minute. "I was slapping at a spider when it happened. The body's in the rug, and Ellis' head rolled past-"

"Is the rest of him up there too?" Donovan patted her faster, his eyes darting from her to the attic. "Is he-"

"Darce, your imagination-"

She cut Wade off mid-sentence. "Imagination didn't put the bruises on my butt when it hit the floor." Darci grabbed her cell from her back pocket and poked at the buttons as fast as her shaking fingers allowed. "I'm calling Max."

"Tell him to send the forensic team," Donovan suggested. When Bradley rolled his eyes, he added, "They have to rope off the place until the coroner takes picture and bags up the body. You know, like on *Law and Order*. Duh."

"Everybody just hold on a minute." Wade grabbed Darci's cell, checked to make sure the call hadn't gone through, then clicked back to the home screen. "Y'all need to calm down. I'll go up and-"

"What in heaven's name is the matter?" Phoebe Clydell was not a woman who would stoop to an undignified run through her home. As her high heels clanked up the stairs to the second floor, Darci couldn't tell whether she was pissed off or alarmed. Her expression was blank, possibly due to the help of a little Botox, but pink tinged her cheeks.

The housekeeper, who Darci only just now noticed gawking at them, moved to whisper something in her employer's ear. The maid pointed to the ceiling, then to Darci, then shrugged.

"Wade Shelton, will you please explain why your wife and her friend are shrieking about a dead body in my attic?" Phoebe's polished red nails tapped a cadence against her crossed arms. Her gaze shifted to Darci. "And what exactly were you two doing up there in the first place?"

Darci felt her eyes widen. "Um, I just...well..."

"We were looking for the bathroom," Donovan blurted. "You have a beautiful home, by the way."

"Yeah," Darci said, glad of her friend's help. "But when I saw it wasn't the powder room, I turned to come back down and that's when the body fell on me. Mrs. Clydell, what do you know about Ellis, your husband's great-uncle? I have reason to believe that's him up there. His head rolled-"

"Darci!" Wade glared at her to get her to hush. He took a deep breath and she could tell he was trying to think of what he should do to get them all out of this mess.

"Sorry, my bad." Bradley stepped forward, looking surprisingly less flustered than the other three. "Must have pointed you in the wrong direction, Darci." He turned to face Mrs. Clydell. "We were busy making those changes you wanted on the floor plans when they came by to take us to lunch. Darci asked if she could use the ladies' room, but I guess I wasn't paying much attention to which way I pointed. It was an honest mistake. No harm done."

"Except that she accused me of keeping dead people tucked away in my home."

Phoebe's comment left them silent.

Darci thought she needed to speak up, but the second Wade saw her mouth open, he stepped in front of her.

"I'm sure this is all just a misunderstanding. You mentioned a spider crawling on your arm, right?" Wade looked at Darci until she nodded, then he glared enough to get her to keep her mouth shut. "She was probably so rattled about the spider, she didn't even know what she was saying."

"Why don't we take a look and see what's wrapped up in that rug, then." Darci didn't want to get the guys in trouble for her snooping, but she didn't like being called a hysterical female in so many words either.

Phoebe huffed, then told Wade to follow her to the attic so they could end the nonsense once and for all. She shot Darci a cold stare on the way past.

They came down a few minutes later. Wade tried to make light of the situation with the lady of the house as he explained to the others that there was nothing wrapped inside the rug, but they'd found a cobweb covered bowling ball a few feet away, obviously what Darci had mistaken for a severed head.

Darci felt like a total moron. Her cheeks burned as she apologized.

"Why don't you two go on to lunch," Bradley suggested. Darci could swear he gave Donovan a look meant to tell him to get the crazy lady far, far away as quickly as possible. "Chuck can pick us up some sandwiches when he goes on a food run for the crew. Wade and I need to work out the details on those changes."

"I'm really sorry, y'all," Darci said, addressing everyone in the room as she headed for the exit.

"Don't worry about it," Donovan said, his voice

full of cheer, trying to salvage things. "It's really pretty funny, once you think about it. Right, Mrs. Clydell?"

"Simply hysterical." Phoebe flashed a sarcastic little smile before she spun on her spiked heels and walked down the hallway, her housekeeper two steps behind.

Donovan talked her into going on to the diner in Dixon, even though she wanted to drop him off at the salon and go hide out in Petal Pushers' workroom.

"I'm such an idiot." Darci covered her eyes with one hand, as if to veil herself from the world, and shoveled chili cheese fries into her mouth with the other.

"No, it'll all be fine. You were just trying to help Ellen figure things out." He took a bite of his Hot Brown. "With your insomnia, the restraining order, and all those responsibilities stressing you out at the shop, that spider scampering up your arm put you on hysteria overload. I totally get how that stuff must've looked like a body in that musty attic."

"I cannot believe I accused a politician's wife of hording corpses." Darci banged her head into the table twice, left it on the plastic tablecloth, and reached for another fry.

"Don't worry about it. Stetson might win elections but nobody is going to nominate him or his uptight wife for any congeniality awards. Tomorrow you'll laugh about the whole episode." When Darci groaned, he added, "Next week then. Now, how are we going to talk the guys into giving us a scaled down version of that awesome closet?"

Darci's Coconut Jam Cake

Ingredients:
French Vanilla Cake Mix
Whipped cream
Coconut extract
Sweetened coconut flakes
Maraschino cherries
Raspberry Jam (Or can substitute your favorite jam or preserves)

Mix the cake according to directions on the box. Stir in 1 tablespoon of coconut extract, then pour into a greased Bundt pan. Bake at the temperature suggested on the box instructions until cake is set, browned, and a toothpick inserted near the center comes out clean. Let cool completely.

Remove the cake from the pan by putting a plate over the cake, then inverting the pan on top of it. Carefully slice through the center of the cake, lengthwise, and gently set the top half on another plate. Spread the jam or preserves over the bottom layer, relatively thick, then replace the top layer.

Ice the cake with the whipped cream. Sprinkle coconut flakes on top and down the sides. Cut a few maraschino cherries in half and use them to decorate the top.

Wipe the extra coconut and whipped cream from around the edge of the plate, if you made a mess like I usually do. Keep the cake refrigerated until serving and between snacks.

This cake looks fancy and pretty, but it's quite simple to make. I like to whip this up when having friends or family over to dinner, and it was a hit the last time I brought it to a potluck supper. Enjoy!

Chapter Ten

*A garden is always a series of losses set against
a few triumphs, like life itself.*
~ May Sarton

"Morning, Darce." Charlotte's smiling face as she
bounced through the door first thing in the
morning brought Darci's spirits up enough for
her to force a grin. "So how'd it go last night? I
almost called at nine to see if Wade bawled you
out as bad as you thought he was going to, but
figured it'd only make things worse if y'all were
actually arguing. How pissed was he?"

"About nine-and-a-half on a scale of one to
ten." Last night Darci fully came to appreciate
her husband's laid back nature. She'd royally
screwed up, but Wade managed to keep his voice
below a yell when he went over the things he
never wanted to see her do again in this lifetime.
"But he'd calmed down by the time I got home,
and bless his heart, he tried not to make me feel

worse than I already did. Not easy, considering I almost got him and Bradley fired."

"Oh no." Charlotte sat down beside her. "I've got to hear this. You know I want details."

"How could I forget? You and Bernice are running neck and neck for Gossip Queen." Darci found that talking about her problems with Charlotte always made her feel better, even in times as bad as this last screw up. "Stetson came storming in yesterday afternoon, probably right after he got a call from his wife telling him all about me making an ass out of myself while I snuck around his house."

Darci felt her ears burning and knew her face was probably beet red, again, over this incident.

"I'm sure it's not as bad as you're making it out to be," Charlotte said.

"Yep, it really is. Wade apologized a million times, told him Bradley and Donovan had nothing to do with my behavior so Stetson could quit dividing his screaming fit between him and Bradley." Darci put her hands on the top of her head and tried to massage her headache away. Didn't work. "Do you have any idea how completely incompetent I feel, having my husband say he takes responsibility for my quote unquote outburst? He actually called it that. My hysterical outburst." Darci laid her forehead against the desk. "Please kill me now."

"Tell me exactly what Stetson said. All of it." Charlotte rubbed Darci's back. "We both know you're not going to be good for anything until you get this out of your system. That's what I'm here for, to lighten your load and make donut runs. Spill it."

"He pretty much told Wade to keep his crazy ass wife off his property or he'd get fired." Darci leaned back in her chair and shook her head. "He said he didn't think much of it when his dad, good ole Charlie, took out the restraining order on me, since the old man's never happier than when he's got somebody to gripe at. That all changed when he found out I went snooping around his house, just a short time after he'd so graciously showed me around Clydell Manor. And he was overjoyed that I accused him of murdering his great-uncle who's been missing since before he was even born."

Charlotte winced. "You actually said that?"

"Of course not." Darci twirled her hair around her finger. "Well, sort of. Hell, I'm not sure exactly what all did spill out of my mouth when I ran out of that attic, except for the part about thinking a dead body fell on me and Ellis' head was rolling around the floor up there." She drew up her knees and hid her face behind them.

"Darce, you remember the time when we were at that party right after we turned legal drinking age? Out on Porter Lane?"

"It's seared into my brain." Darci peeked up at her. "But what's that got to do with anything, except it was pretty funny."

"That's my point. It's funny now, but I thought my life was over after that night." Charlotte flashed a mischievous grin. "How was I supposed to know Billy Blake was going to move his pickup

199

when I was right in the middle of peeing out all the beer I drank. Not a good time to wear overall shorts. And then he stopped with his headlights shining on my ass."

Darci couldn't help but laugh as the scene re-played through her mind. "You were so drunk, you didn't even realize what was going on until everybody turned away from the bonfire to laugh and whistle. I'll never forget the look on your face. The only time you couldn't play it cool."

"You ran over and held up a beach towel until I pulled up my drawers, then brought me home while I cried in your passenger seat, telling me things weren't nearly as bad as I thought." Char-lotte propped her elbow on the armrest.

"You told me to shut the hell up, if I remember right," Darci said, smiling.

"But now we both see the humor in it. Don't forget," Charlotte said, tousling her own short blonde hair. "Because of that über-embarrassing moment I met Jimbo, and now we're married and have little Cole. If Billy's headlights weren't shin-ing on my naked drunken butt, he wouldn't have tossed you the towel he'd been sitting on when you ran past. When I returned it to him the next week, that's when he asked me out. So Cuz, good things can come from humiliation."

"At least nobody saw my ass." Darci laughed, and felt a little better. She hugged Charlotte. "Thanks for being here for me. And for not peeing on my petunias."

"What about your insomnia?" Charlotte asked, moving on to another subject. "Getting any better?"

"Well, the nightmares about the shop getting blown away in a tornado finally stopped." Darci fidgeted with a stray piece of raffia.

"Gee, Darce, you looked so thrilled about it."

"Now the dreams are about . . . I think . . ." Darci bit her lip, searching for the right words, wondering whether she should even verbalize what she thought her dreams were.

"Come on, spit it out." Charlotte's sarcastic tone calmed to one of concern. "What's bothering you?"

"I'm dreaming about what happened to Betsy's husband, I think. Guess my brain's on overload with everything that's going on. But it was just so vivid. Bright colors, and I could feel the grass and sticks under my feet when I ran through the woods in the nightmare."

"Tell me all about it. You're as a pale as a ghost."

"Funny you should say that, since Miss Addie was in the dream too. It started off with her standing beside a cabin motioning for me to join her, but with her finger up to her lips," Darci said, pausing to illustrate the shush gesture, "so I'd be quiet."

"Was she all decked out in ghost garb, with mist around her and stuff?" Charlotte's eyes grew wider as she spoke, then they darted around the room as if she expected Miss Addie to pop into view.

"No, pretty much like she looks when we get a glimpse of her here. But she was solid, like she was still alive. It was night time, the window was open, and when we looked through it, there was a woman on the floor in the corner, her back to the room. I heard babies screaming, that's when I saw the little feet sticking out under her elbow. She was trying to protect them, keep herself between them and the others."

"Damn." She had Charlotte's full attention. "Then what happened?"

"An older man and a teenage boy pointed guns at her. They were yelling, but I couldn't make out what they said. Then a man burst through the door and struggled with the other two. The gun blast was so loud my ears still rang when I woke up this morning. The man dropped dead, but the other two seemed devastated, even though one of them pulled the trigger. They ran to him, cradled his head on one of their laps, and shook him like they were trying to wake him up. That's when Miss Addie got Betsy's attention. She motioned for her to get the hell out while they were busy with the guy I'm guessing was her murdered husband.

"She ran through the door with the babies. Miss Addie took one of the little girls, grabbed Betsy's arm, and lit out running like hell. Betsy tried to turn back at one point. Miss Addie shook her real hard and said she had to save her children. I trailed behind them and after a few minutes, we heard footsteps behind us."

"Then what?" Charlotte asked.

"They ran a while. Miss Addie seemed to know where she was headed, kept pointing out logs and rocks not to trip over. Then we heard shots whiz past us. Miss Addie pushed Betsy down behind some briers, made the sign for her to keep quiet—I think I was invisible to them both at that point—and told her to hand over the shawl she had on. She gave the baby back to her mother, then took off running with the shawl and the baby blanket."

"Oh my God." Charlotte shook her head. "No wonder you can't get any rest, with dreams like this."

"You should have seen it. I was scared to death. Took me a while to figure out whether to stay and watch over Betsy and the twins, but I opted to chase after Miss Addie. She ran through thick weeds until she got to the river. We heard more gunfire, and she picked up a big rock and threw it in the water with the shawl wrapped around it. Paxton would've been jealous of her pitching arm. Then she tied the blanket around a chunk of driftwood and hurled it in.

"Another shot came from behind us. My heart stopped when Miss Addie let out the most blood-curdling scream I've ever heard. She wasn't hit, though, thank goodness. She yanked off her shoe and pitched it in the river, then ran off through the trees. In the dream I was frozen to the spot, trying to scream but couldn't. Last thing I saw before I woke up was that baby blanket floating down the river, bobbing on the waves in the moonlight."

"I can see why that shook you up. You think that might be what really happened?"

"It felt so real, not like other dreams, any dream I've ever had. Maybe it was, or maybe it was just me thinking about the mystery in my sleep. Don't guess there's any way of knowing." Darci rubbed her arms, trying to get rid of her goose bumps.

Class night meant rearranging the workroom after the shop closed. Darci and Charlotte had eaten an early supper, chicken salad sandwiches and Pepsi, and were just about done setting things up.

"Teaching these classes is a lot more fun that I thought it'd be." Darci placed a stack of handouts beside a bowl of vermiculite and glanced around the room. "What makes me nervous is I don't know if I'm qualified to teach anything, and I just don't want to mess this up, especially now that I need the extra money the course brings in. You know what I mean?"

"I do. You feel like you're in over your head, like one day somebody is gonna walk in to call you out on being an impostor, like you're just pretending to know what the hell you're doing." Charlotte crossed her arms. "That's how I feel every time little Cole cries and I don't know what to do. Until last year I'd never been alone with a baby, now I'm supposed to be trusted to raise one myself. Hell, somebody really should make a parent test or something before they let people go off birth control. I just got the hang of how to warm up the baby wipes, then yesterday the pediatrician tells me kids are getting potty trained earlier than ever. How the hell am I supposed to figure out how to teach a little boy to tinkle in a potty? I'm so gonna screw that kid up." She looked a little embarrassed at having said more than she'd meant to. "But you don't have anything to worry about, Darce. You're great at what you do, and too damn stubborn to ever give up."

"I'm sorry, I didn't even ask how you were making it with the teething." Darci kicked herself for being so thoughtless. She'd been meaning to ask to keep Cole all weekend pretty soon, to give Charlotte a chance to catch up on her sleep or have some fun. Ashley babysat whenever Charlotte needed her, but Darci also knew she felt guilty ⟨wasting the sitter's time', as she'd put it last month, unless she was coming to work or had errands to run that weren't baby friendly. She let the grandparents each have the kid overnight once a month, during which time she and Jimbo would go out to a restaurant, maybe a movie or bar with a live band, where her cousin would spend half the time checking her phone for emergency calls that thankfully never came. Darci remembered going through the exact same thing when Paxton was a newborn. "You're an awesome mom, you have to know that."

"Adequate at best, but thanks. At least I'm glad Jimbo still thinks I look hot, even with stretch marks." Charlotte making jokes was a good sign. Darci hated to see her sad or worried. "Teething's going much better, since we keep his little gums either greased up with Orajel or half frozen with this new textured freezer thing that looks like a dog toy. Now he only wakes up once a night."

"Well that's better."

"It's always at two a.m."

"Not great timing, but an improvement from when he squalled every three hours around the clock and neither one of you could get a wink of sleep." Darci'd felt so bad when she walked in and saw Charlotte asleep at the counter one afternoon, pen in hand.

"Last week I actually dreamed my gynecologist gave me this new purple pill. Promised that if I took it, it'd make Cole sleep eight full hours every night from then on, no matter what, through colic, teething, thunderstorms, chicken pox when he got older, even rabies. I popped two of those suckers and had the best sleep of my life, woke up in the morning with little blue birds chirping outside my window, the sun streaming in through my lacey white curtains." Then Charlotte grimaced. "That's when I really woke up, with Cole screaming his head off because he'd had explosive diarrhea during the night, which leaked out of the cheap bargain diapers Jimbo bought at Discount City. All over him, his crib sheets, and even spattered on the wall."

"That sucks."

"Tell me about it." Charlotte rolled her eyes, her ruby red lips pursed before she grinned. "I went from daisy fresh to scrubbing shit before I even got my hands on a coffee cup. That was not a good day."

The students arrived at Petal Pushers on time, with their sleeves rolled up and ready to learn. Tonight's class covered propagation, so Darci started things off by asking everyone to take a few cuttings from a spindly Wandering Jew and put them in a jar of water with their name on it in the workroom window.

Later, during their break, she and Charlotte brought up Betsy and Ellis, to see if any of the ladies just happened to know any hundred-year-old gossip that might help.

"Do they have a copy of the will you mentioned?" asked Tilly Cooper.

"No, but Ellen said she hoped the genealogist would be able to locate it soon, in case it had any more information about Ellis, and to see if what Betsy said about the clause was right." Darci nibbled at one of the donut holes she'd picked up at Krispy Kreme for refreshments. If she chewed each bite enough times, maybe that would burn off the calories it took to eat the little snacks.

"Give me that guy's name again." Tilly turned over her instruction sheet, pen poised. "I work in the courthouse one door down from where they keep all those old records. Won't take me ten minutes to trot in there and see if his will is on file. It might save your friend a little time and money."

A few days later, Darci found another twig with

leaves and tiny florets, this time beside the coffee pot when she went for a refill. How it got there she didn't know, but pieces of this plant kept turning up around the shop. She'd just opened her mouth to yell for Hoyt, to ask what he knew about it, when the phone rang.

"Darci, I just had to call and let you know what I found!" Darci had never heard Hattie sound so excited. "You'll never guess, not in a million years."

"Well, don't keep me in suspense. I'm on the edge of my seat here, literally." Darci wasn't lying.

"Remember when I mentioned Grandma's cookbook, and that I planned to get around to reading it that weekend?" Hattie asked.

"Yes," Darci answered.

"Well, Gene ended up dragging me off to a swap meet, so I didn't get around to it til this morning. You know, she stuck all kinds of neat stuff in that recipe book of hers." Hattie chuckled, and Darci hoped she didn't sidetrack into nostalgia land too far, since she was dying to know what she'd found. "Clippings from the county paper, church bulletins, there was even a yellowed ole coupon for SPAM sandwiched between recipes for yellow cake and ambrosia salad."

"Huh, didn't know SPAM has been around that long." Darci wanted to be polite, but the suspense was killing her. "What else was in there?"

"The little memo book Grandma kept her midwife records in! It was tucked in toward the back in the pie section. I tell ya, there were tears in my eyes when that little jewel landed in my lap, literally, and I realized what it was." Sniffles through the receiver suggested that Hattie was probably dabbing her eyes with a hankie about now.

"Oh my goodness. That's incredible!" Darci was so excited, knowing what a sentimental treasure the discovery was for Hattie, plus she hoped Betsy and the twins were mentioned in its pages. "Have you read it yet?"

If Hattie decided to savor the moment by putting it off a few days, Darci would have to lay the phone down, run out in the yard, and scream her frustration to the blue jays.

"Yes, I've poured over every last word and scribble the better part of the day," Hattie said. "It's really interesting. The front section is full of information Grandma must've wanted to keep handy. Stuff about herbs for a healthy pregnancy and to prevent miscarriage, a sketch for turning breach babies, lactation enhancers. Then there's a page of scriptures, the one to stop bleeding, that kind of thing. The bulk is taken up with her delivery records. She brought quite a few babies into the world."

"Did you find Betsy and her twins in it?"

"They're there, but," Hattie paused as if searching for the correct words to use, "it's a little strange. It's set up in columns that go across both pages when the memo book is open. The date, the mother's name, father's name and then the baby's, gender, health, birth weight, a concerns column where she wrote stuff like no milk or weak cry. The last one on the right side is labeled notes."

"Midwives had so much responsibility back then, doing an obstetrician's job without benefit of medical school. It's sort of the 'in' thing again. About half of the ladies in Charlotte's Lamaze class last year said they were using midwives and doulas." Darci thought she might even consider going that route, if she and Wade ever decided to add to the family. "Sorry, didn't mean to side-track you."

"Oh that's fine, dear, Now where was I?" Hattie paused and Darci heard papers rustle. "Betsy's entry. It has them here, born August 8th, 1905, identical twin girls. Says 'tiny, check on often.' But the weird thing is that Betsy's last name has been marked out, along with whatever was in the note column. Looks like the original entries were done in fountain pen, which faded to a brown shade with age, but this is blacked over with a newer pen, maybe ballpoint. Whatever was in the father's column is blacked out too, no surprise there, but this would suggest to me that Grandma came back years later to blot out the names."

"That is weird," Darci agreed. "I get what you mean about the different ink. With what we know about Betsy's husband dying and them having to run, I'd have understood if Miss Addie hid the paper trail right then, but why would she have waited years down the road to blot it out?"

"I have no idea." Pages flipped in the background again. "The other thing I wanted to mention is a page toward the back. Here it is," Hattie said. "Labeled little angels at the top. This is where she recorded stillborns and infants who died a day or two after they were born."

"That's so sad. Must have been the only downside to bringing all those babies into the world." Darci visualized Miss Addie's little angels, and knew it must have broken her heart each time she'd had to write on that page.

"What stuck out to me is an entry in the middle. It's dated three days after Betsy's girls were born. That's when her husband died, right?"

"Yes, August 11th." Darci was on the edge of her seat once again, this time fidgeting with a paper clip, unfolding it and absentmindedly bending it into various shapes.

"That's what I thought." Hattie went on. "Ellen needs a copy of this. Maybe I can make Gene go over to the drug store this evenin' to run off copies for everybody. He's sure to do it, especially if I bake his favorite peach cobbler and tell him he has to pick up the vanilla ice cream while he's there. Can't have peach cobbler unless it's a la mode."

"You've got my stomach growling." Darci hadn't made time for lunch, since she was so worried about getting wedding flowers done on time. "I don't understand, though. Somebody had a stillborn the day Ellis died?"

"No, but the date is what caught my attention. There's no mother's name for this entry, but it says Ellis, first name only, in the father column. My thinking is that Grandma wanted to mark down the event, and she didn't come back to black anything out. It simply lists the date, his first name, and that's all. Oh, she drew a bunch of little black birds in the note column and colored 'em in. Odd that she picked this somber page to doodle on."

"You're right," Darci said. "She must have felt the need to commemorate his death, and put Ellis in that column to show he was the father that passed. Wouldn't it have been something if she'd have written exactly what did happen to him?" She didn't want to hurt Hattie's feelings or lessen the importance of her discovery. "I'm just glad you found proof Ellis died on the day Betsy said he did."

They hung up after Hattie promised not to cut a slice of cobbler until Gene made copies. She'd get them in the mail first thing in the morning, or else her husband would starve out in the doghouse.

Cuttings
Class handout

Starting new plants from cuttings is a terrific way to save money and fill those empty pots. It's the easiest way to propagate, and you'll have extra plants to give to your friends.

What you'll need
Plant cuttings
A pot filled with vermiculite OR a small jar filled with water

Take cuttings from your favorite plants. A section four or five inches long from ivy or a wandering jew, with the lower leaves taken off, or a single leaf from something like an African violet. Either put the cutting in the water (submerging the bottom section but not the leaves) or set the cut end firmly in the vermiculite and keep moist. Roots should form in a couple of weeks, and then you can repot your new plant in a pretty container.

List of a Few Plants to Root from Cuttings

African violet
Begonia
Butterfly Bush
Christmas cactus
Clematis
Coleus
Crepe Myrtle
Geranium
Honeysuckle
Hydrangea
Ivy
Jade Plant
Primrose
Rubber Plant
Sage
Viburnum
Wandering Jew
Weigela
Yarrow

Chapter Eleven

Don't wear perfume in the garden—
unless you want to be pollinated by bees.
~ Anne Raver

"You look puny again, Darce." Charlotte continued her circuit around the shop, watering the potted plants. "I thought those mugwort pills were helping you get over your insomnia."

"It's still working. Now if I could find some way to quit having weird dreams, maybe I could actually get some rest while I'm asleep." Darci sipped on her second cup of coffee, eager for a caffeine jolt that had yet to arrive.

"No more nightmares, I hope." Charlotte wiped water droplets from the marble top table in front of the porthole. "If the Ghost Lady is in another one, you ought to get her to tell you what the deal is. See if she could help you out."

"She was only in that one, but Betsy and the twins are always there. Asking questions probably wouldn't work, like when you try to scream and can't, or like when you try to read in a dream and the letters are all scrambled up. Oh, or worse, when you're trying to run away from a monster but your feet move like they're stuck in taffy." The thought of candy made her stomach rumble. She was definitely exhausted, since she'd been too tired this morning to eat before she left the house. "I've had this dream every night for the past few weeks."

"Well, go ahead and tell me what happened. Might make you feel better." Charlotte stood on the other side of the counter, leaning her elbows on it.

"Sure you want to hear about it?" No way could she discuss this with Wade or Max, since they'd both be pissed if they knew she was still helping Ellen with the whole Ellis thing.

"You know I do."

"It's just weird. Vivid though. It's sunny outside, the sky's all blue with big fluffy clouds, and the treetops and grass are the most vibrant shades of green you can imagine. I could even smell the fresh early morning breeze. Betsy's standing in the woods, one twin in the crook of each arm. Tobacco leaves are at her feet, spread out real neat and on purpose. She's holding sprigs of those leaves I keep finding on my desk, but like a bouquet, and they morph from little white flower clusters to purplish berries, then to colored leaves, over and over. I can't understand what she's trying to tell me. The only word I did pick up on was beware."

"Just a second. Be right back." Darci slid a sketch to Tilly Cooper before she stood to greet the two teenagers who'd just walked into the shop.

"Is Hoyt working this afternoon, Darci?" Amber asked. Ashley Rosales, her friend as well as Cole's babysitter, stood beside her. The girls were just getting used to Darci's order not to call her Mrs. Shelton. She'd rather feel like they thought of her as a girly type instead of a matronly ole Missus. Even if she knew she was deluding herself. Most teenagers thought of twenty-four as over the hill.

"Sure is, out loading up the van. You can go on back, if you want." She thought a lot of both girls, who giggled as they traipsed through the back door. Ashley's long brunette curls swung behind her.

Jimbo was home with Cole today, so she guessed the kids were probably planning something fun for when Hoyt got off in half an hour.

"Sorry about the interruption, Tilly." Darci sat back down beside her, ready to go over the plans she'd drawn up to landscape the Cooper's side yard, the big bonus responsible for drawing even more customers to sign up for gardening classes. "Is this the kind of grape arbor you had in mind?"

"Yes, it looks perfect. The bench underneath will be a great place to sit in the shade and have lemonade while the kids play." Tilly tapped the sketch with her forefinger. "This groundcover underneath. You sure it'll hold up to being walked on?"

"That's Irish moss, hard to kill and easy to grow. We'll leave plenty of extra space between the flagstones for this to fill in." Darci reached for a sample in a small pot and passed it to Tilly. "That's about as tall as it gets, so you won't have to trim it back. Blooms in little white flowers in the spring, about the same time as Easter flowers come up. The other drawing shows what the whole thing should look like as the seasons change."

Designing with plants was one of Darci's favorite things to do, and she was pretty proud of this arbor plan. The new focal point in the Cooper's yard would provide a shady seating area which would grow enough grapes to keep Tilly's little girl and boy full of jelly sandwiches in the coming years.

"I love this, and can't wait to get started!"

"How about next weekend, maybe Saturday afternoon?"

"Let me check my schedule right quick." Tilly reached into her purse, then pulled out a couple of papers folded in half along with her calendar. "I was so excited to see what you'd drawn up, I plum forgot to give you this." She plunked the papers down on the table between them. "What you mentioned in class the other day."

Darci unfolded them and glanced at a copy full of old-timey handwriting. "What is it?"

"I know, antique cursive is kind of hard to read

at first, huh? That's Titus Clydell's will," Tilly said, more interested in the sketches she couldn't take her eyes off of than the document. "I found it in the records department this afternoon."

After they agreed on a time to do the work that weekend, Tilly left Darci reading over the will. She scanned it into the computer, emailed Ellen, and then printed out two copies, one to mail to Hattie and the other for herself to make notes on.

Sure enough, Betsy was right about there being an inheritance clause for Ellis and his descendants. Darci underlined it, then ran her finger down her copy, looking for something. She found it at the bottom and checked it against her notes.

The will had been signed August 8th, 1921, sixteen years to the day after Betsy's twins were born. She couldn't help but wonder about the significance of the date.

Darci had enough time to read through the whole thing once more before she had to close up the shop.

I, Titus Herbert Clydell, being of sound mind and a fairly healthy body, leave this as my last will and testament. I wish to be laid to rest in the family plot alongside my parents and my dearly departed wife. An account has been set aside for my burial, incurred expenses, and my headstone.

My beloved wife Camilla passed on to the great beyond many years ago. She and I had only two children, one of which has been a great comfort to me in my advanced years. For that reason, I leave most all of my worldly possessions to Terrence Elvin Clydell, including my home, its contents, and all my property and investments not men-

tioned in the following. He may take possession as soon as I am deceased, and is held to honor the following clause to the fullest letter of the law.

I add this in regards to my eldest son, Ellis Milton Clydell, absent from me though always present in my thoughts and heart. A disagreement caused us to part ways, at his choosing. It is my sincere hope that he finds his way back into my life before this document is put to use. Since that will most likely not be the case, I find it necessary to include the following stipulations. It would grieve me greatly to think that Ellis and his children would have to do without their fair share of my legacy. I decree that the sum of twenty thousand dollars be put in a trust fund, to be distributed to and only to Ellis Milton Clydell and/or his legal heirs. Also, I wish to allot a tract of land to go with the above mentioned trust fund. There is a large acreage of land behind Clydell Manor, mostly wooded at the time of my writing this. Those fifty-two acres are to be held for my boy Ellis, in the event of his return, or the return of his progeny. This land is not to be leased, sold, chopped up into lots, or drastically altered in any way, shape, or form until it is claimed. If my son, Ellis Milton Clydell, does not come to sign the papers in person, proof must be given to show beyond a reasonable doubt that the progeny that collects is indeed my blood relation through Ellis. In that case, an attorney chosen by Terrence or his heirs will be hired to oversee the proof, et cetera, and will be repaid in full for their service with a sum deducted from the trust fund.

I do understand that the funds and land aforementioned cannot be held indefinitely through the ages. It grieves my heart to even consider the possibility that this stipulation might need to be added. Sadly, I feel it prudent to add this, so these holdings never fall to some other end.

The funds and land set aside for Ellis M. Clydell will remain in trust until the advanced date of the year twenty-twenty (2020). If at that time no one has came forward to collect on behalf of my beloved albeit estranged son, this inheritance, plus all interest and increase *added through the time span, shall revert to the living descendants of Terrence E. Clydell.*

This is my last will and testament. So be it.
Titus Herbert Clydell
August 8, 1921

Darci's gaze moved from the document to the bowl of fruit on the counter. Her stomach growled to remind her she'd skipped lunch to finish filling an order. The big green apple drew her attention, and she fantasized about impaling it with a Popsicle stick—or maybe a twig from a tree outside, like she'd seen on Pinterest—then dipping it in ooey, gooey melted caramel. Dark chocolate drizzles would come next, then a roll through a plate of chopped peanuts and pecan chips. Crushed M&Ms would be good to finish off a deluxe candy apple, and she was sure that would be Paxton's favorite. She jotted down ingredients to pick up on the way home, grabbed the big green apple, and trotted off to the kitchen. Right now she'd just make due with chocolate syrup and sprinkling it with crumbs left in the bottom of the cookie jar.

Mrs. Jenkins sat in her usual chair by the hall doorway, sipping on a glass of sweet tea, a lemon slice clanking again the cubes. She'd came in to buy some annuals to replace the impatiens that dried up in the heat. Darci knew Mrs. Jenkins often forgot to water her flowers, as evidenced by some she'd returned to the shop, and talked her into replacing the everyday bloomers with hardier drought tolerant begonias, which should look pretty in the terracotta pots that accented each step up to her tidy front porch.

The coral pink flowers waited by the register while the ladies finished visiting. When Mrs. Jenkins drank the last of her tea and was ready to check out, something on the counter drew her attention.

"I didn't think those turned color until later in the year." She picked up a sprig of leaves, green turning to yellow and red, with a cluster of small dark blue berries. "I always thought these bushes were so pretty, especially in the fall."

"You know what that is?" Darci asked. She'd been looking through her plant books and on gardening websites all morning, trying to identify it. This was the umpteenth time she'd found pieces of this plant on her desk. The fact that she'd seen leaves and berries exactly like this in her dreams made her try even harder to figure out what it was, in case it actually was some clue as to what happened to Ellis. Nobody else had access to the shop after she closed or before she unlocked the door in the morning, except the ghost. She couldn't figure out what Miss Addie was trying to tell her. "Somebody sent that to me, looking for its proper name, but I can't place what it is."

"It's a variety of Viburnum, I believe." Mrs. Jenkins held it near her glasses for a better look.

"It's a cousin to Possum Haw, but that has red berries instead of this indigo color."

"Viburnum . . . give me a second here." Darci typed the genus into the Bing search box. Sure enough, varieties of the bush popped up on screen. Darci clicked to the first site listed and quickly spotted leaves and berries identical to those she'd found earlier beside her phone. The plant boasted a showy cluster of white flowers in early summer, which turned into pink berries that ripen to dark blue a few months later. Shiny oval leaves started out dark green before they turned a beautiful mottled yellow and maroon in late fall. There was a shot of it in the snow, all leaves gone, the berries the birds hadn't eaten on woody black stems.

"You're right, *Viburnum nudum*." She stood up and smiled at her friend. "Thanks so much for telling me, and saving me no telling how much time figuring it out."

"Glad I could help." Mrs. Jenkins glanced back at the sprig held in her weathered fingers. "You know, these bushes used to line the driveway over at the Clydell place. Oh, you wouldn't believe how pretty they looked in the fall. I used to walk by there on my way to school when I was a little girl. Broke my heart when they tore 'em out. That Charlie never did have good sense."

Charlie Clydell was the last person Darci wanted to think about right now, but she tried to keep her emotions off her face. "I wonder why he got rid of them. I don't think anything borders the driveway now."

"Who knows, but that's one of the first things he did after he inherited the place when his daddy passed." Mrs. Jenkins looked like she was lost in thought. "Could you order me a couple of these bushes? I'd love to watch them bloom from my porch swing."

"You bet I can." Darci made a note on the pad on the counter. "They'll be my gift to you, for helping me answer . . . that person's question, about the genus species."

Later that afternoon, Darci rested her back while she checked the email. She jumped to her feet as she read the first one she clicked open.

"Charlotte, come here!" Darci stood pointing at the computer screen. "You're never going to believe this."

"I work in a haunted flower shop. What's going to surprise me," she wisecracked.

"Remember me telling you I couldn't understand what Betsy said in the dreams? Well a couple nights ago I woke up right after another one. That time I heard flute music in the background, which reminded me of the Pow Wow, so when Betsy spoke, I remembered listening to the Native American storyteller. I'm a moron for not getting it before. She was talking to me in Cherokee. Duh!"

"Cool dream, but that's not really earth-shattering news."

"Well, the next part might impress you. I woke up with it fresh it my mind and wrote it down phonetically as best I could. The only Cherokee person I know is Sue, so I emailed her right then, before I could chicken out. That was two in the morning, and the funny thing is, I laid down and slept like a baby the rest of the night." Darci sat down in the chair. "For the first time in months."

"Your friend is gonna think you're nuts." Charlotte put her hand on her cousin's shoulder.

"Wrong!" Darci pointed at the screen and gloated a little. "I asked if she could translate a line I heard in a movie that stuck in my head. Didn't want it to be a total lie so I said I'd been hearing it in my dreams ever since. This is her answer. Betsy was saying, 'The weakness of our enemy makes our strength.' It's a Cherokee proverb!"

"That is so weird! Our ghost must think it's pretty cool too, since she just laid one hell of a cold spot on us." Charlotte rubbed her arms. "Nothing like freezing to death in July."

"Tell me if you think I'm nuts but-"

"You are, but go on."

"Ha ha. Seriously, this has to be a clue. No way can a dream in a language I don't understand, spoken by Miss Addie's BFF in a serial dream, be a coincidence. Could it?"

"I looked up mugwort after you had that first nightmare and told you it said vivid dreams are a possible side effect." Charlotte shrugged. "But, that doesn't explain the translation. You think our ghost could be putting ideas for the dreams in your head? Like when you got the urge to research her family the day before Hattie first walked in here last year?"

"At this point, I believe anything is possible."

Darci cupped her hands theatrically and spoke to the room. "Miss Addie if you're responsible for that dream, you need to do a crayon drawing for me in the next one, because I'm not smart enough to figure this thing out."

She really wished she could go to Max with the mounting clues, but knew he'd probably holler at her again to stay out of it. The last time she'd brought Ellen up in conversation with Wade, he asked if she needed any construction done up in Pennsylvania, so he could get something lined up for when all this Betsy business got him fired.

Petal Pushers Plant Profile for Viburnum

Viburnum nudum
Perennial shrub

Viburnum is also called Possum haw and smooth witherod.

Brief description: This perennial shrub grows 3 to 6 feet tall, has glossy oval dark green leaves that turn red and maroon in fall. Clusters of white flowers bloom in April and May, then turn into pink berries that ripen to a dark blue shade.

Growing instructions: Grow in full sun to partial shade. Prune only as needed in the fall.

Uses: These grow best in groups, for pollination, and look pretty in shrub borders and beside water gardens. This plant is absolutely beautiful in the fall, with its blue berries and vibrant red leaves.

Chapter Twelve

*It is good to be alone in a garden at dawn or dark
so that all its shy presences may haunt you
and possess you in a reverie
of suspended thought.*
~ James Douglas

Darci broke the hamburger meat apart in her skillet with a big wooden spoon, then tossed in a handful of chopped red onion to give the sloppy joes a flavor boost. Homemade oven fries baked in the oven, and the smell made her stomach rumble.

"How's the homework coming?" Darci opened the jar of sloppy joe sauce, to have it ready to add after draining the fat off the meat.

"I don't see why they have to give us homework on our first week back to school." Paxton let out a long huff to show his irritation. "Almost done, just have to finish this stupid English lesson over plurals."

"Let me know if you need any help." Darci readied the plates, silverware, and napkins on the counter. Dinner wouldn't be for another fifteen minutes or so, but she liked to save time, and hoped to put her feet up while the potatoes finished browning.

"'Okay. Mrs. Merriweather put in some tricky ones," Paxton said as his pencil scratched across the worksheet. "Like moose and deer are what we're supposed to say whether there's one or fifty, not deers with an 's' or meese, like Angie Turner said and got it wrong. Do you know what to call a bunch of lions? It's not pack, 'cuz Jake asked about it in class, but the teacher wouldn't give us any hints."

"Ha, heard that on Jeopardy last week, lucky for you." Darci grinned at him as she sliced a fresh tomato from the backyard, a pretty heirloom one, golden yellow with red stripes. "It's a pride of lions."

"Thanks." Paxton wrote that on the blank line. "The bird ones are the weirdest, like gaggle of geese. Bet you'll never guess what a group of crows is called?"

"Hmmmm. When they sit in a tree above my car and poop all over it, I call them a name that'd get you in trouble." She winked at her son, whose eyes were dancing as he waited to tell her the right answer. "Never mind that, though. I give up, how am I supposed to refer to a gathering of black birds, crows I mean, next time I run across one?"

"It's a murder! No kidding," Paxton said as he

shoved the papers into his folder, then returned it to his backpack for school the next day. "That's what Mrs. Merriweather said a bunch of crows are. At least that one should be easy to remember."

"I never hear that before." Darci put the lid on the sloppy joes after she slid the skillet off the hot burner. "Guess that's another reason black birds are in so many horror movies. Time to go get washed up."

Darci was in the workroom getting materials ready for the class scheduled to meet that evening. Even though the idea sprang from her need to raise money to pay for the greenhouse, she was surprised by how much she enjoyed teaching. When the bells on the front door jangled, she put a stack of handouts on the table and walked up front.

"Hey Max." Darci hugged her favorite lawman. "Did you stop by to brighten up my day," she paused to pull back and search his face, "or is something up?"

He wasn't smiling. This couldn't be good.

"We need to talk, if you've got a minute."

"Sure. I'll get Hoyt to watch the register." She hollered for him, then headed to the kitchen. "I'll meet you out back with some lemonade, if you want to warm up a seat on the bench for us."

"Bench better be in the shade," Max said, lifting one corner of his mouth in a grin. "Don't

231

skimp on the ice or we'll both melt."

Darci walked outside a few minutes later, a knot in her stomach as she worried about what was wrong now. At least it wasn't urgent, since he had time to wait under the big oak tree for her to bring refreshments, so she knew nobody was hurt or dead. Probably. She handed Max a glass, condensation already beading on the sides, and sat down next to him.

"Okay, so what's the matter." Darci wished she had a lemon Krispy Kreme to go with her drink. Chewing usually helped calm her nerves.

Max took a deep breath and slowly blew it out. "I spent the last hour talking to Stetson Clydell." His left eye squinted as he pointed his gaze at Darci, a look that had meant she was in deep trouble when she was a kid. "About you."

"I already apologized for that. Well, I left one on his voice mail, since he wouldn't pick up any of the four times I tried to call him. I know confusing a bowling ball with a dead person was pretty stupid but-"

"You've got to quit all this nonsense," he said, his hand held up like a crossing guard with a stop sign. "Stetson came to my office to talk to me about filing charges against you. Criminal charges for harassment, trespassing, slander, and possible endangerment. I thought we talked about you staying clear of the Clydells after the restraining order, but from what I hear, you plum forgot all about that."

"Oh my God, Max, are you here to arrest me?" Panic set in. Darci felt her lip quiver as her heart slammed against her ribcage. "Harassment, tres-passing, I don't think I did any of that stuff, not on purpose anyway."

Max's expression softened a little. "No, kid, I'm not gonna throw you in the pokey. This time. Have you talked to Bernice or Vera Thompkins today?"

"No. Why?"

"Because Charlie Clydell ended up lying on his back with one of those big concrete planters on top of him. After they got it off him and settled him down, he called his lawyer, to sue you and Petal Pushers for negligence since you took the things to Golden Days." Max took a sip of his lemonade, then held the glass up to his forehead. A breeze ruffled the leaves overhead, but did little to make the August scorcher any cooler. "Lethal landscaping."

"Is he alright?" Charlie was a miserable old coot, but she didn't want him to get hurt. "I don't understand how it could have fell on him, unless a tornado came through. Those planters are heavy, even empty."

"Here's the deal. Four of his buddies were out-side with him, but instead of them moving the thing off poor Charlie, they sent somebody in to get help. Stetson said he knew his dad orches-trated the whole thing, since there wasn't even a scratch or bruise to be found on his old keister, but since you were recently in his attic acting like a nut, he thought it might be a good idea to re-port it, just in case."

"That's a relief. Sort of, I guess." Darci relaxed

233

into the bench until another thought entered her mind. "What about the other stuff he wanted you to arrest me for?"

"Lucky for you, the trespassing would never stick, since his housekeeper let you in. If he wanted to press charging you with harassment and slander, you'd have a problem. You were in the man's house hollering about a dead body, asking his wife what Stetson knew about his great-uncle's disappearance. If that's not bad enough, you've got Bernice and Mabel grilling everybody at the nursing home about the same damn thing." A frown pulled at his salt and pepper brows. "This kind of rumor could screw up the man's chances in the election. He doesn't deserve that."

"I'm sorry about handling things wrong at his house, but Max, I really think they're hiding something. Ellen and her family just want to find out what happened to their great-grandpa, and what's responsible for a family secret that spanned four generations. We're almost positive he was murdered, and from what Betsy said about running from her husband's family, it had to be one of the Clydells who did it."

"You're gonna have to keep those ideas to yourself." Max hadn't talked to her in this stern tone in almost fifteen years. "None of that makes any difference, everybody's dead now who could've done it anyway, though I seriously doubt that's the case."

"All the evidence points to it being true. The marriage bond, the birth log, and I've had this feeling-"

"That's enough!" Max's voice echoed through the yard like thunder. "What in the world's wrong with you? Your imagination's run wild and you're about to get yourself in serious legal trouble I won't be able to get you out of if you don't let this go. If Charlie keels over from old age or anything else when you're anywhere near him, I guarantee Stetson'll have a legal team throw you under the bus, not to even mention if he catches you snooping around again. Let your friend Ellen work on this by herself. Or she can explain to Paxton why you're in jail the next time you pull a stupid stunt."

"Ten more minutes." Darci poked the snooze button without even opening her eyes. The same dream, with a new opening, had looped through her head all night, replaying over and over, which left her as exhausted as if she'd really trotted through the woods all night long. If she could doze for just a couple minutes . . . .

When the alarm buzzed again, Darci sprang awake. Agitated, she grabbed the pen and paper from her nightstand and jotted down a page full of details she didn't want to forget. She almost tripped on two crayons on the floor beside her bed; how they got there, she didn't know, since Paxton thought he was way past the coloring book stage.

Wade didn't have to get up yet, so she tried to

be extra quiet as she tiptoed to the bathroom, stepped into her jeans, and pulled her hair into a sleek yet sloppy up-do secured with a ponytail elastic, a trick Donovan showed her one day when she looked a hot mess.

As she ate a quick breakfast, she mentally went over the dream one more time. This last one started out differently. It'd felt like she was watching a movie when she saw Daisy fly over Clydell Manor. For some reason that hadn't made her nervous, even though they kept the parakeet's wings clipped for fear of her darting through the door. Daisy flew through the woods behind the mansion, but then, right when Darci thought the bird was going to land on Betsy's shoulder, Daisy exploded into a group of crows.

A murder of crows, to be precise.

From the drawing Hattie found in Miss Addie's midwife log beside Ellis' name, along with the information they'd documented and her gut feeling, everything pointed to Ellis having been murdered. Darci was convinced, when she wasn't doubting her sanity, that the first vivid dream had shown her what actually happened, though there was no way to prove it. But she had asked the ghost for a hint.

Now, after that last nightmare, she thought she knew where to look for the body. Black feathers had rained down on Betsy as she spoke in Cherokee. One ebony plume, marred by a thick drop of blood, landed on the bouquet of mottled leaves in Betsy's hands. Then it drifted into the ground at her feet.

"Thanks, Miss Addie," Darci whispered. "For sketching it in crayon."

Darci watched the sun rise with a shovel in her hand. Summer rain from the previous week had softened the ground under the layer of old leaves and pine needles from nearby trees. Otherwise, she never would have gotten this far.

Wade should be waking Paxton up before long, then take him to school on his way to work.

When her insomnia had been at its worst, she'd taken long walks before dawn in hopes of wearing herself out enough to sleep when night rolled back around, and if the exercise helped her lose a couple pounds in the process, even better. That's what Wade thought she'd been doing the past three mornings.

When Darci'd figured out where she thought Ellis' body was, she'd told Charlotte her plan and sworn her to secrecy.

It was a shame she couldn't tell Hoyt what was going on. She'd have been willing and happy to pay him double overtime to help her at this early hour, since he was quite a bit faster with a shovel than she was. But she couldn't risk anybody finding out what she was up to, and Hoyt had a bad habit of letting things slip out of his mouth before he remembered they were a secret.

No one could find out until she had proof. She'd already gotten herself in enough trouble. If Stetson Clydell had any notion about her trespassing in the woods behind his house, he'd not only pitch a blue fit, he'd have her arrested for sure. He shouldn't be able to see her, unless he decided to go for a long walk at sunrise, which, thankfully, he hadn't done. A thick growth of weeds stood between the pit she was digging and the manor, good camouflage should anyone wander past. Actually her feet now stood about four or five feet deep in the hole. The rope she tied to a tree yesterday hung down behind her, to serve as a way to pull herself up.

That first morning, she wasn't surprised when she'd walked straight to the spot she'd seen in the nightmare. A *Viburnum nudum* grew where Betsy had appeared in the dream, its pink berries turning to blue amidst the oval leaves, the only bush of its kind anywhere to be found in the vicinity. Unless she was woefully wrong—or just plain full of shit, as Max would've said if he knew what she was doing—that shrub served as a headstone over Ellis Clydell's grave.

The rotting layer of foliage held in the dampness from recent storms. The first day she'd only removed a foot or so of dirt in the four foot square area. How she'd managed to decide how big to make it she didn't know; this just felt right. The second day she'd snuck out of bed even earlier to excavate a few more feet of soil.

She hoped it wouldn't take much longer. A thunderstorm was supposed to come through that evening and if the hole filled up with rainwater, she'd be screwed. No telling how long it would take to dry out. Charlotte was going in to

238

Petal Pushers early to cover for her today, so Darci told her she was going to stay here as long as it took. She figured if she dug more than six feet and didn't find anything, she'd have to admit she was wrong.

This deep, she tried to be careful each time she put weight on the shovel. She didn't want to sever any of Ellis' body parts as she dug, and knew the murderers would never have had time to get a coffin. Then she realized that after a hundred years, nothing would be left of the poor guy but his bones, even if they'd covered it with plastic, if plastic sheeting even existed way back in 1905. She shivered at the thought, but kept going.

The shovel blade thunked against something. Darci squatted down to see what she'd have to move out of the way this time. Probably another tree root, and if so she'd have to climb out for the Black & Decker battery-powered alligator lopper she'd hidden behind a nearby log. Anything but a giant rock would be okay.

Her hand made contact with something solid, an object too broad to be a series of tangled roots. She used a trowel to move the loose soil out of the way. It looked like the top of some sort of box, and after a little more dirt got moved aside, she realized she was kneeling on top of an old trunk. Her mom kept a similar one in her living room. Darci figured this one held human remains instead of quilts and blankets.

She climbed out of the pit and moved the rope out of the way, then whipped her cell phone from her pocket to call Max . . . but stopped with her finger poised over the call button. He'd probably start hollering about how she didn't have any business digging up Clydell property and for her to get her butt out of there, pronto. Maybe she should open the trunk first, to make sure she had proof before she got Max on the phone. She tucked the cell back in her pocket. Thing was, she didn't think she should disturb the crime scene by opening it. That was a big deal on the crime documentaries she watched on Sunday afternoons.

Peering down at what she felt certain was an open grave, she struggled to decide what to do. Maybe she could have Wade call him. "Yeah, right." Wade would be just as pissed, more so because she'd lied about where she was, what she was doing, and that she'd stay the hell away from his construction site to keep from getting him fired. She leaned over further, still talking to herself. "If I get the lid open, I could snap a picture of the skelllllllllll-"

Clumsy should be her middle name. She'd leaned too far and fell into the hole. At least she landed on her butt instead of breaking her neck.

As she moved to get up, she realized the trunk lid had busted when she landed on it. She scooted over and her hand went through the now cracked slats between the metal pieces meant to give the antique luggage strength when it traveled by wagon or train.

"Oh no." Fabric. She felt fabric. If she'd spent this much time only to find some lady's old long lost bloomers, she'd go bang her head against the nearest tree until she knocked some sense into it.

She pulled the material through the crack and found herself staring at a rotten sleeve.

Arm bones were still inside it.

"Ha, I knew it!" Touching skeletal remains hadn't freaked her out nearly as bad as she'd imagined. Darci had gone out of her way to help Ellen, risked being arrested, made a spectacle out of herself and pissed a bunch of people off, based mostly on her gut feelings. DNA tests could prove this was Ellen's great-grandfather, and Stetson could kiss her sweet Southern ass if he didn't like it.

Now that she had proof of a murder—or a hidden body at the very least—she decided to put that call through to Max.

"Uh-oh." Her phone came out of her back pocket with a broken screen.

"Damn, it won't even come on." Shaking it didn't help. She reached for the rope, which wasn't there, since she'd moved it out of the way when she climbed out. "Damn, damn, damn! Maybe if I'd lost a little weight like I'd planned, the stupid phone wouldn't have broken when my big butt fell on it." She took a deep breath to calm herself down, then tried to figure out how to get out of the grave.

Charlotte knew where she was. If she didn't show up at Petal Pushers for lunch, she'd come looking for her. Wouldn't she? Darci sure hoped so.

She sat down to wait.

Something moved. Darci must've kicked a

piece of rope with her foot.

"But there's no rope down here, that's why I'm stuck." Darci jumped up as mortal fear took over. The sun was shining down on her through the trees, and when she worked up the courage to look down, she saw it. Copper and tan, with hourglass shaped blotches.

"Snake!" She clawed at the dirt walls to no avail. "Shit on a biscuit!"

Petal Pushers Plant Profile for Snapdragon

Antirrhinum majus
Annual

Snapdragons are also called Toad's Mouth.

Brief description: Snapdragons have spikey flower stalks that come in a variety of colors including pink, yellow, red, and white. Annual bedding plants usually grow from 6-18 inches in height, while some varieties can reach two and a half feet.

Symbolism: Snapdragons represent deception and graciousness.

Trivia: Antirrhinum means 'like a snout' in Latin, and snapdragons are said to look like the snout of a dragon or calf. The flowers look like opening mouths when pressed on the sides, then they snap shut.

Growing instructions: Snapdragons grow best in full sun to part shade. Remove faded florets to encourage more blooms.

Uses: Snapdragons work great in mixed borders and make pretty additions to bouquets.

Chapter Thirteen

*Gardening is civil and social, but it wants
the vigor and freedom of the forest and the outlaw.*
~ Henry David Thoreau

"Help!"

She clasped her hand over her own big mouth. What if Stetson heard her? He might kill her to shut her up. This rotting corpse would definitely not help his campaign efforts. In her peripheral vision, the snake slithered across the broken lid before it disappeared inside. Good thing Ellis was already dead or she guessed he'd have died of fright.

If she stayed in the hole, that thing would eventually bite her. Tears trickled down her face and she couldn't catch her breath. Things she'd Googled about venomous snakes flashed through her mind: triangular heads and elongated cat-like pupils. Who the hell wanted to get close enough to see those details? She didn't care whether or not the snake was poisonous. If venom didn't kill her, she'd die of heart failure.

She frantically clawed the walls, failed to find a toehold, then weighed her options. Scream and risk Stetson strangling her to death. Hush and get snake bit.

The snake or Stetson?

Stetson came from a family of murderers, she reminded herself, when she realized he was winning over the creepy crawly snuggled up to his Great-Uncle Ellis.

Stetson or the snake?

She opened her mouth to scream, but the sudden cold spot she found herself in shocked her silent. She exhaled again. Vapor formed in front of face, as if she'd been smoking a cigarette or standing in a deep freeze.

Could it be? And if so, could she help?

"Miss Addie, if you're here, please help me." The words came out a shaken whisper.

Nothing could stop the scream that escaped Darci's lips when she felt something wiggle on her head, then drop around her shoulders as she slapped at it. Another snake must have fallen right on top of her.

Then she saw what it really was. The rope! The one secured to the tree. Hanging in front of her were the knots she'd tied herself. But this wasn't possible. Out of habit she'd moved the rope over to the base of the tree so she wouldn't trip on it. How did it . . . ?

"Thank you, Miss Addie."

Darci shimmied out of the grave quick as

lightning--into another cold spot where she thought she detected the scent of lemon verbena--before she ran for her house

An hour later, Darci watched the coroner take pictures of the open trunk, before and after Max and his deputies lifted it out of the hole she'd dug. One of the officers had laughed at her for being so afraid of a snake, but changed his tune when Max put him in charge of getting rid of the nearly four-foot-long copperhead.

After she'd ran home, Darci had called Charlotte to tell her to close the shop and drag Max to the dig site if she had to. She'd drawn a map that showed exactly where it was before she tackled the job. The quickest shortcut meant parking on the side of a gravel road and walking north through the woods until they either saw the open grave or fell in it. After a quick shower, her hair still dripping wet but filth free, she drove down the road and parked at the designated spot five minutes before Max pulled in with Charlotte seated beside him.

"Darci Odette Shelton, your imagination better not be runnin' amuck again or I'll take you in myself, young lady." Then he'd surprised her with one of his bear hugs. "You okay?"

"Shaken, but fine. Now grab your crime tape or whatever and follow me." Darci started off, but he grabbed her arm.

"Think I'll take a look-see before I break out

the yellow tape," he said, sarcasm in his voice. "When Charlotte came bursting into my office, she said you'd just shimmied out of Ellis Clydell's grave, which you just happened to find waaaaaay back behind Stetson's house. That right?"

"Yep, with a snake to hasten my climb out." Darci'd been eager to show him, and didn't want to waste take time explaining her actions. "Come on."

"Okay, but you'd best be right about this. I knew you weren't just speculating, if it was important enough for you to close Petal Pushers for a few hours," Max said as the three set out, Darci leading the way. "Guess you were pretty sure about all this, seeing as how you totally ignored me chewing you out over staying the hell away from the Clydells."

After Max laid eyes on the cracked trunk with the skeletal arm sticking out, he'd called the station, which brought deputies and a medical examiner soon after. That's when he sent a deputy to the manor to let Stetson know what was going on.

"You understand Stetson isn't to blame for this, right?" Max had already apologized for not giving any credit to her gut instincts, even though Darci fully understood the position she'd put him in after the attic episode. "Promise me you're not going to yell at the man or grill him about who did it."

"I'm not a moron, you know. Stetson wasn't even born when all that went down, or his grumpy daddy either." Darci was proud to have actually figured this whole thing out. "Everything points to the murderer being Titus or Terrence Clydell, the dead man's father and little brother."

"You finding the body doesn't mean you've won the Scooby Doo Badge of Crime Solvers, you know." Max laughed as he took his memo pad out and clicked his ink pen. "But give me your theory. I'm all ears this time."

Darci had gone over what she'd tell Max a bunch of times in her head. After proving she wasn't a hysterical lunatic, she needed to be careful not to mention the ghost, though she wasn't sure how to explain how she got out of the grave without mentioning her. She rehashed everything, starting with Hattie finding Miss Addie's midwife log and the notation with the murder of little crows beside it, which backed up Betsy's bedside confession about Ellis' kin being responsible for his death and trying to kill her and their twin daughters.

"Titus, who'd be Ellis' dad and Stetson's great-grandpa, didn't want any Indians climbing into his family tree. I don't know what possessed Ellis and Betsy to come to Webster County when they did, though my guess is he thought his family would open their hearts when they met the woman he married, especially with her pregnant and about to pop. Didn't happen though, since Miss Addie Brown's records list the babies' birth in a ramshackle cabin instead of that great big house over there."

"How do you know it was Titus who shot him? Prominent as the family is, he could've hired it done." Max waited for her reply, pen poised.

"Um. . . ." Darci had to be careful not to mention the dream in which she saw Titus and a teenaged Terrence—who she remembered clearly from the portraits Stetson, the spitting image of him, had shown her in Clydell manor—point guns at Ellis, heard the gunshot, and watched both of them fall to their knees in grief. That might put her back in the nutcase file. "You know, maybe they tried to scare him into sending her away, and the gun accidentally went off. That would make a little sense, given the circumstances. But that doesn't excuse him trying to kill his granddaughters and their mom. Being a senator, congressman, whatever he was at the time, and as mean as the snake that scared me crapless earlier, the only option in his mind might've been to shut them up for good. Nobody would likely vote for a man who shot and killed his own son, or let his other son pull the trigger, whichever the case."

Charlotte stood behind Max. She gave Darci the thumbs up and winked, her way of congratulating her for telling a believable rendition without the prophetic dreams, the ghost, or the bush sprigs that magically appeared on her desk.

Max turned around while Charlotte's thumbs were still up. He cocked his head.

"Good job, um, figuring all that out." Charlotte crossed her eyes when Max turned back around.

"Back up a minute." Max flipped back through his notes. "Did Betsy say Titus shot at them too, or just ran 'em off?"

"Uh . . ." Darci purposely bit her tongue, literally, the only way she kept herself from telling Max she didn't think it was Titus who killed Ellis. Her money was on Terrence, regardless of his age at the time of the murder. That would explain why Miss Addie was so enraged when she mistook Stetson for Terrence last fall, when she went all poltergeist on him with the paper cut and door slamming.

"She died before she could spit out the whole story." Charlotte answered that time, since Darci stood there having a duh moment over what to say. "All Ellen and the family know is that she thought somebody from their great-grandpa's family would hurt her girls if they found them."

Max stepped aside to answer his cell, which gave Charlotte a chance to speak to Darci in a private whisper.

"Guess now that Cherokee proverb makes sense. 'The weakness of our enemy makes our strength'. Titus' weakness was burying his son in his back yard, so to speak, and putting that clause in his will. The burial was over his remorse, his weakness."

"Right." Darci nodded. "And the will that covered his ass was our strength, and a great clue to boot. It guaranteed nobody would stumble on his son's grave, since the property couldn't be legally altered until years after Titus died."

"I still wonder how those Cherokee words came through so clear in your dreams," Charlotte said. "Since Addie and Betsy were so close, you don't suppose-"

Max joined them again at that moment, so they had no choice but to change the subject.

No surprise when Stetson showed up a minute later, huffing and puffing from walking so fast. After he explained who he was to the deputies, one of them asked him what he knew about the situation.

"I swear I don't know a thing about it." Stetson's flabbergasted expression was priceless, especially in comparison to his usual political persona. "Only thing my dad ever said about Uncle Ellis was that he ran off because Titus didn't like his girlfriend. And he warned me about treasure hunters, as he called them, trying to scam a claim to the money Pappy Titus set aside in his will. He said some old bitty showed up doing just that years ago, but my Grandpa Terrence took care of it, set her straight. I figured that was the main thing that worried Daddy when Ellen and her bunch started asking questions. That's all I know, I swear. Now can we cordon off the area, to keep this from leaking out to the press? I mean, we don't know for sure who Darci just dug up. Plus, she isn't even supposed to be here in the first place."

For some reason, Stetson's words made Darci shiver in spite of the heat.

"Tell you what, Darce, why don't you go on back to the shop. I'm sure the thought of that closed sign is making your skin crawl." Max knew her well. He glanced at Stetson. "No need for you to deal with him right now. I'll call you later."

Non-Toxic Weed Killer

I don't like to use poison chemicals on my plants, especially in my vegetable garden. Lots of people don't like to use commercial weed killer because they worry about their children and pets getting sick from playing outside after they spray.

Try this instead!

Vinegar will draw the moisture out of plants and weeds, turning them to a dried up brown in a few hours. Use vinegar full strength or dilute with a little water. Either use a squirt bottle or sprayer to zap weeds around your yard and garden.

It will kill your pretty flowers if it gets on them, so aim carefully.

Chapter Fourteen

*Give me odorous at sunrise a garden of
beautiful flowers where I can walk undisturbed.*
~ Walt Whitman

"Pax, you and Jake go wash your hands," Darci yelled to the two little boys who ran through the shop. "We eat in two minutes."

"Thanks again for inviting us here today," Ellen said as she peeled the plastic wrap off a plate full of deviled eggs. "Don't know how I'll ever thank you for everything you've done." She nearly choked Darci with another big hug.

"Told you to stop saying that." Darci hugged her back. "Glad to help. Too bad Hattie couldn't make it, since Gene's back was acting up again."

Charlotte walked into the kitchen, baby Cole on her hip sucking on his fooler. "We're ready for the food. The tablecloths are on the picnic tables, Bernice and Mabel have the plastic forks and napkins arranged all neat and nice, Donovan's sweet tea is poured. Picnic's ready as soon as we get the eats outside."

"Everybody grab a platter and let's go then." Darci took the fried chicken, praying she didn't trip and spill the food she'd spent the morning cooking, then picked up the dressed bananas Bernice and Mabel made.

Ellen followed with the deviled eggs and fried green tomatoes. Charlotte brought up the rear with the potato salad, and Cole helped by trying to knock the bowl out of her hand.

The *Viburnum nudum* she'd ordered for Mrs. Jenkins sat beside the greenhouses. The classes she taught to help pay off the debt from replacing that structure had gone so well, she had another course planned for fall, and sales from those heirloom veggies and flowers brought in even more than she'd hoped. Now she could look at the greenhouses with a sense of accomplishment instead of visualizing dollar signs swirling down the drain.

As they ate, they rehashed the reason for the picnic celebration. After they covered the part where Darci tried to claw her way out of the open grave to get away from the corpse and the copperhead, she quickly moved on to more pleasant details. She shuddered each time that snake crossed her mind, plus she kept having to remind herself that the story these people knew left out Miss Addie coming to the rescue with the rope. She still didn't understand why she'd smelled lemon verbena when she'd crawled out of the pit, since Miss Addie's perfume was a combination of rose and vanilla.

"I can't explain the emotion I felt when the DNA came back with a match." Ellen put another deviled egg on her plate. "To have proof Betsy was right, to realize what her life must have been like guarding that secret all those years. Now their souls can be at rest, if you believe in that kind of thing."

"Gotta tell ya the truth," Shane said around a bite of chicken. He swallowed and wiped his lips on a napkin. "I thought it was a waste of time getting the cheek swab. I mean, what are the chances of all this, right? Ellen, Trish, I'm glad you two had the gumption to pursue this whole thing, and Darci proved Ellis Clydell was our great-grandpa. Could you pass the biscuits please?"

"I'd still like to choke Charlie, that old fart!" Bernice wiped a few stray crumbs into her hand and put them on the side of her plate. "Causin' all that fuss, lyin' about the planter falling on him, not to mention cussin' Darci out. And he knew the whole story all along!"

"Could've saved." Mabel, shy around this many people, covered her lulls in speech by tapping her neatly folded napkin to her lips. "So much trouble. Old coot."

Max had taken Stetson with him when he went to question Charlie about the body, since Charlie had owned the property for a while when he inherited it from his father. Neither his son nor the sheriff were prepared for what he told them. The sedative he'd taken before they arrived might

have been responsible for his acting less belliger-
ent than usual. Who knows, maybe it was a relief
to finally get the truth off his chest after a lifetime
of harboring the secret.

Charlie told Max and Stetson what his daddy,
Terrence, had sworn him to secrecy about so
many years ago.

"My daddy was just a teenager then, when him
and Pappy Titus tried to scare off that Injun Ellis
took up with. They didn't know anything about
his dealin's with her, til he brought her around
all knocked up. It turned my grandpa's stomach,
and he just got more put out when she dropped
twin girls. One would've been bad enough. Anyhow, they went to scare that woman and her
brats off, but Ellis came back early and caught
'em trying to force his wife to take the first train
out of town and never come back, to Dixon or her
husband. Ellis charged at 'em, since they were
both pointing guns at that Injun and her spawn.
Titus' pistol went off on accident." Charlie paused
a few seconds and shook his head. "Daddy said
he'd never forget the wail his Pappy let out when
Ellis bled out and died in his arms."

"Accident or not, may they both rot in hell for
what they did next." Bernice was outraged about
the incident, as they all were.

Charlie had figured he might as well tell the
rest. "Cain't nobody get in trouble now, after all
these years. Isn't my fault what went on back
then. Daddy and Pappy Titus chased after that
woman when she ran off. Yeah, she really gave a
damn, high tailin' it out of there before her hus-

band let out his last breath. They couldn't have her tellin' tales about the accident, what with Titus in the running for governor right then. He said they'd most likely have paid her off, like their original plan, and scare her real bad, but she fell in the river before they had a chance. Daddy said they saw one of the babies floatin' off on the current. Problem solved. Don't give me that look, it was for the best and you know it." He'd directed that part to his son. "Imagine if that happened to you."

Max said Stetson turned lily white at that comment, but told his dad to finish the story. He wanted to know why, if they thought Betsy and the girls were dead, did Titus leave the clause in his will.

"He was a sly ole fox, Pappy Titus was." Charlie had let out a belly laugh. "He buried Ellis smack dab in the middle of the acreage he set aside for the heirs he thought were already dead. Nobody would be alive to tell the tale after the hundred years or so were up. That way the land couldn't be sold, or plowed up, or anything else, so there wasn't much chance of the grave ever being found." Then Charlie'd frowned. "Guess now that brood'll put up teepees and sell moonshine, once the deed's in their names."

"To his credit," Max said, leaning back and adjusting his belt to hang lower over his full stomach, "Stetson got up and left then without a word. Charlie stuck his lip out and pouted. I asked him if there was anything else he ought to tell me.

259

"He got all haughty with me then," Max said, mimicking both the expression and voice Charlie had used. "Screwed his face up and said, 'Folks need to mind their own b'ness, or else they get what's comin' to them for botherin' the Clydells.'"

I swany, that whole bunch ought to be run out town before they hurt anybody else. Isn't two murders enough? My head's about to split in half, and I cain't bear the thought of Darci a-getting' hurt if that Clydell walks through the door again.

I'm gonna have to come up with a way to let that lawman in on the facts. Those Clydells took somethin' precious from me, and I haven't been the same since. My ole brain gets a little foggy over the details, but I have to set things right. Lord knows it's time.

There has to be a way.

At least maybe Ellis is at rest now. And I'm so glad Betsy was there to help Darci out.

Darci stared at her plate and she chewed a piece of fried chicken. She'd been surprised to learn Titus was the shooter instead of Terrence when Max first told her. Probably a good thing it wasn't Terrence, since there's no telling what sort of psychological effect a teenager would've gone through after killing his own brother. She shuddered to imagine the warped individual he might have grown into, had that been the case.

"Hey, I just remembered something," Darci

said, making eye contact with Ellen. "That morning we found the . . . um, Ellis, Stetson said Charlie had told him some woman came around a long time ago trying to collect on Titus' will. You don't think that would've been Ella or Emma, or maybe one of your moms, do you?"

"No, they would've told us something like that." Ellen shook her head. "I know it wasn't Betsy, either, since she was too scared to set foot back in this state. Charlie sounds like the paranoid type, so maybe he didn't have all his facts straight."

"Yeah, you're probably right about that." Darci cut another wedge off her fried green tomato and stabbed it with her fork. "At least that explains why Stetson looked funny that day I met with him, when I mentioned the will. Maybe he thought we were a bunch of gold diggers. Anyway, glad we've got that all settled."

"I know. Stetson was nothing but cordial when we met with him to sign the deed," Ellen said. "We were kind of expecting him to be pissy about the whole thing, but instead, he invited us back to the manor, took us on a tour and everything."

"If we hadn't popped up, he would've eventually been able to cash in the trust fund set aside in the will. That twenty grand has grown quite a bit, with the added interest, since Titus arranged this so many years ago." Trish shook her head. "That's what we thought would've really made him mad, but like Ellen said, he was nice as pie."

Shane spoke next. "We decided to put most of it aside for our kids. Probably just keep out enough to cover what it costs to bury Ellis beside Betsy, and get a new headstone for the both of them. With their real names this time."

"Got a little surprise for y'all about that." Darci leaned back and smiled. "Celia Kemp called me a few times after I found the grave. Word about that leaked out pretty quick, as big news in a small town usually does."

"I told my men to keep it quiet," Max added. "But no tellin' how many people saw the ME's vehicle get loaded with what any fool would've guessed were remains, even in the box we put the trunk in."

"I called Stetson to tell him about her questions, since she'd told me he'd answered her with a big 'no comment' before he hung up on her." Darci smoothed out her napkin. "He insisted on paying for the reburial, headstone, and I do believe he mentioned a catered get-together after the service."

"You're kidding," Ellen said. She, Trish, and Shane looked like they couldn't believe it as they exchanged glances with each other. "He didn't mention it the other day. Wonder what made him decide to be so generous?"

All eyes turned to Darci.

"I didn't talk to him until yesterday," she explained. "You see, he nearly pooped tulips when I mentioned the local paper. The election is almost here, so his tone with me turned to butter, telling me he didn't want the scandal to get out since most folks won't vote for a politician with a skeleton in the closet, much less one with a murdered great-uncle buried out behind his house. That's when I said I wondered if I might be able to convince Celia that someone buried in the Clydell cemetery, which really wasn't that far from the burial site, was being reinterred in a separate family plot beside his wife at the request of his descendants."

"You've never heard a man agree to anything so quick." Charlotte laughed. "Darci had him on speaker phone, so I had to leave the room to keep quiet after he agreed to Darci's terms in exchange for that story."

"Ah, that makes more sense," Trish said. "You don't know how much we appreciate all this Darci."

"Oh, y'all should've heard him when I mentioned how much extra time I had on my hands to spend talking to Celia, what with me only being able to go to the retirement home on Tuesday mornings." Darci still couldn't believe she'd had the nerve to say that, something just this side of blackmail. "Stetson fell all over himself then, and promised to have the restraining order Charlie took out on me dropped, withdrawn, whatever the right legal term for it is, before the sun went down. That was my icing on the cake."

"Hey Mom, speaking of cake," Paxton said, "can we have dessert now?"

Darci and Charlotte brought out double fudge brownies and peach cobbler still warm from the oven. Wade scooped ice cream on top of the dessert, and one little scoop in a plastic dish for Jimbo to feed baby Cole.

As she passed dessert plates around, Darci couldn't help but smile at how lucky she was, surrounded by friends and loved ones she wouldn't trade for anything. She marveled at the extraordinary circumstances that had brought them all together.

She heard Daisy's cheerful singing through the open screen windows.

Life really was one big miracle.

Dressed Bananas

Ingredients:
Bananas
1 package of vanilla pudding, made according to directions on box
Chopped peanuts

Do one banana at a time, so they won't turn brown before they're coated.

Cut each one into thirds. Roll the pieces in pudding, then the peanuts, and put on a plate to serve.

Great accompaniment to any meal or picnic, and makes a healthy snack. Leftovers keep for about 2 days in the fridge, but are usually gobbled up way before then.

Plant and Recipe Index

Acknowledgements

A big thank you to everyone from TheNextBig-Writer for their support, advice, encouragement, and help, especially Nathan B. Childs and Patti Hauge. I also want to thank the Louisville Romance Writers and the NaNoWriMo community.

Most importantly, thanks to my family for putting up with me: Amanda, Brittany, Tyler, Barry, Tommy and Jan Cole, and Bobby and Edna Brown.

About the Author

Photo courtesy of Brittany Hayes

Tina D.C. Hayes writes romantic suspense and cozy mysteries. She lives in western Kentucky with her husband and three children. A few very pampered pooches and two parrots keep her busy, but guard against writer's block.

http://tinadchayes.wordpress.com
http://twitter.com/Tina_DC_Hayes